I0823804

RED STAR REBELS

ALSO BY AMIE KAUFMAN

The Isles of the Gods Duology

The Starbound Trilogy (with Meagan Spooner)

The Unearthed Duology (with Meagan Spooner)

The Other Side of the Sky Duology (with Meagan Spooner)

Lady's Knight (with Meagan Spooner)

The Elementals Trilogy (for children)

The World Between Blinks Duology (with Ryan Graudin, for children)

ALSO BY AMIE KAUFMAN AND JAY KRISTOFF

Aurora Rising (Aurora Cycle_01)

Aurora Burning (Aurora Cycle_02)

Aurora's End (Aurora Cycle_03)

Illuminae (The Illuminae Files_01)

Gemina (The Illuminae Files_02)

Obsidio (The Illuminae Files_03)

Memento (The Illuminae Files_0.5)

RED STAR REBELS

AMIE KAUFMAN

ALFRED A. KNOPF
New York

A Borzoi Book published by Alfred A. Knopf
An imprint of Random House Children's Books
A division of Penguin Random House LLC
1745 Broadway, New York, NY 10019
penguinrandomhouse.com
getunderlined.com

Library of Congress Cataloging-in-Publication Data is available upon request.
ISBN 979-8-217-02901-3 (trade) — ISBN 979-8-217-02903-7 (ebook) —
ISBN 979-8-217-22785-3 (int'l ed.)

A brief portion of this work was originally published in different form in the short story "One Small Step," which appeared in *Begin, End, Begin: A #LoveOzYA Anthology*, published by HarperCollins Australia in 2017.

The text of this book is set in 11.5-point Dante MT Pro Regular.
Rocket launch art by alones / stock.adobe.com

Manufactured in the United States of America

1st Printing

The authorized representative in the EU for product safety and compliance is Penguin Random House Ireland, Morrison Chambers, 32 Nassau Street, Dublin D02 YH68, Ireland, https://eu-contact.penguin.ie.

Random House Children's Books supports
the First Amendment and celebrates the right to read.

For Matt and Jack

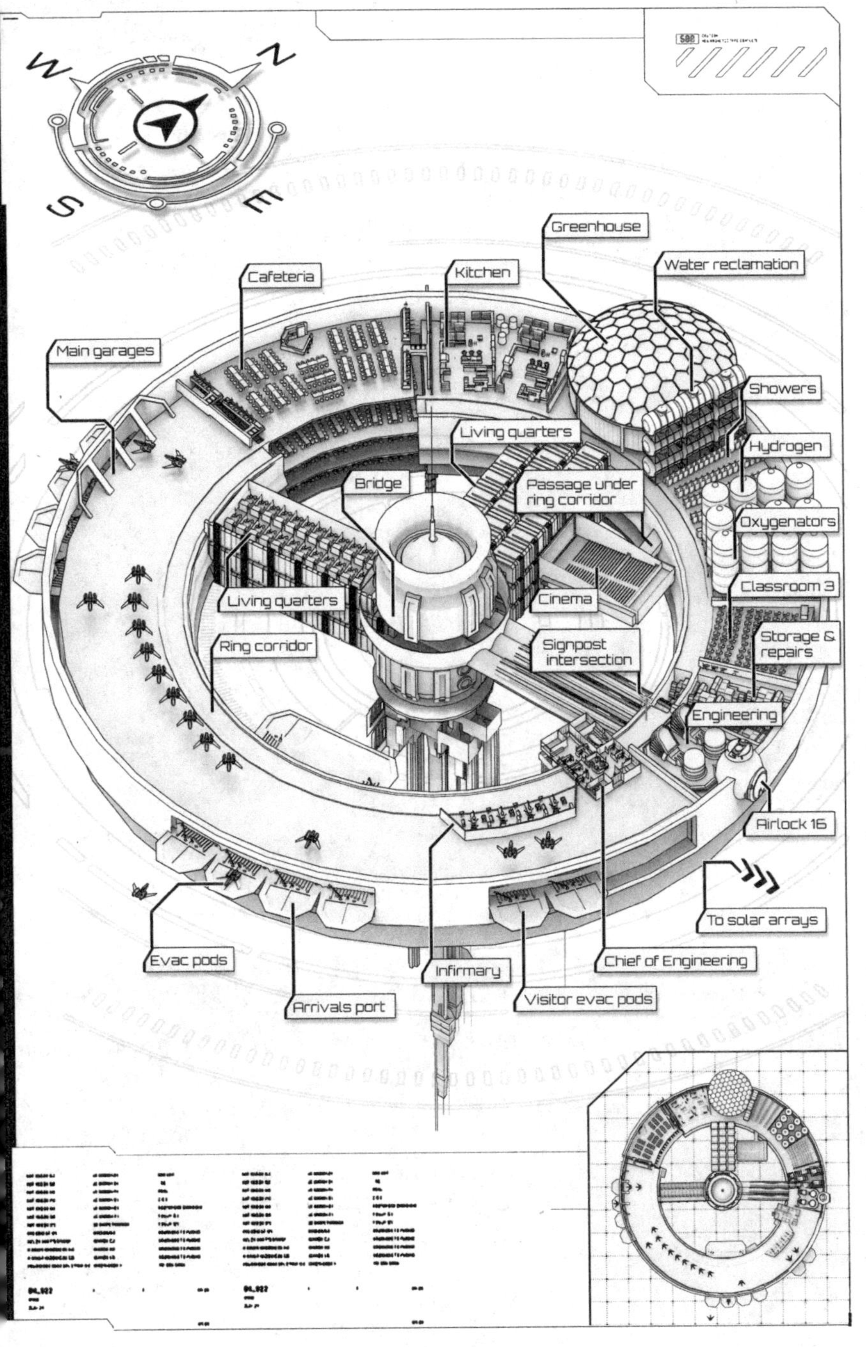

W
N
S
E
Greenhouse
Water reclamation
Cafeteria
Kitchen
Main garages
Showers
Living quarters
Hydrogen
Bridge
Passage under ring corridor
Oxygenators
Living quarters
Cinema
Classroom 3
Ring corridor
Signpost intersection
Storage & repairs
Engineering
Airlock 16
To solar arrays
Evac pods
Infirmary
Chief of Engineering
Arrivals port
Visitor evac pods

TIMELINE

1960s	First Mars flybys by USA and Soviet Union. Hey hey, Mars!
1971	Soviet Union successfully lands Mars 3. Transmission ceases after 14.5 seconds. Still a win!
1976	USA lands Viking 1 and Viking 2. Pictures and data successfully transmitted. Woo!
1980s–2020s	Multiple successful unmanned landings. But why do robots have all the fun?
2036	Michael Graves and GravesUP Industries launch a surprise mission. First humans land on Mars. Wait, what?
2040s	USA, Russia, China, and India rapidly launch missions, in contravention of the United Nations Outer Space Treaty.
2045	United Nations Pax Mission lands on Mars, attempts to assert authority. Ha, nice try, nerds.
2056	Fiftieth settlement established on Mars. It's getting crowded up here.
2067	PRESENT DAY

1.

HUNTER

8 HOURS REMAINING

THE GUY FROM MARS didn't know I was coming.

"Hi?" he says, with an upward inflection that asks who I am, what I want, and why I'm standing here when he's already checked everybody off his list. I can tell he doesn't like loose ends. Messes up his filing system, probably.

He's guarding the airlock with a tablet in one hand, wearing a United Nations jumpsuit and a confused expression. I'm not sure what kind of formal processing I expected, but this is an underwhelming way to arrive on a new planet.

This guy is here to welcome diplomats and corporate officers from all over Earth and the orbital colonies before they shuttle down to the surface. You'd think the UN would have laid on whatever flourishes they could manage for our arrival, but instead it's me and one nervous bureaucrat called . . . I squint at his badge. NATHAN, apparently.

"This is the shuttle, right?" I prompt. "All aboard for Mars?"

"I thought I had everyone already," Nathan says, frowning at his tablet, then looking up at me with a narrowed gaze, as if I might be a hitcher. "What's your destination?"

I unleash a smile on him. Never hurts, right? "I'm here to transfer to the GravesUP compound."

"Then nobody at GravesUP knows you're coming. I've logged in everyone expected for this shuttle."

True, Nathan. My mother and sister have no idea I'm on the way. Warning them would have meant giving up my advantage, and I didn't spend four months lying about my location, crammed into a tin can of a freighter and eating meals out of foil pouches for nothing.

"It's a change of plan," I explain, which has the benefit of being true. "The captain was saying there's no rides from Orbital down to the Graves compound today because of a dust storm. She thought I could get a lift to the UN base—to Pax—and then have my guys send a rover over to pick me up."

"We'll figure it out." Nathan sighs, like a man used to nobody respecting paperwork the way he does. "Got a name?"

I actually look down at myself, as if my body might have somehow transformed while I wasn't looking. I literally can't remember the last time this happened.

Our parents always kept our faces out of the newscasts—the best way to keep safe is to be unrecognizable. But I don't spend much time with the general public, so occasionally I forget that most people don't know me on sight. Everyone I encounter in my daily life sure does.

I've never been a fan of *don't you know who I am?*, but it's going to be hard to avoid it this time.

"My name's Hunter Graves."

"All right, let's see if there's a free seat. I gotta tell you, that dust storm's messed up a lot of people's plans," he says, tapping at his screen as I mentally count down.

Ten, nine, eight . . .

"Actually, the dust has nearly reached Pax too, but we should be able to—"

. . . seven, six, five . . .

He looks up. He blinks. "I'm sorry, did you say *Hunter Graves*?"

There it is.

"At your service," I reply.

"As in . . . as in *Graves*?"

As in, this is basically my family's planet, is what he means. We were fastest. We were first. And everything here, including the orbital platform we're standing on, runs on GravesUP systems.

"That's me," I tell him, hefting my bag on my shoulder in a subtle show of impatience. "Pleased to meet you, Nathan."

The bag isn't uncomfortable. It weighs exactly ten kilos—or at least it did on Earth. It'll be three-point-something on Mars. I took the standard personal effects allotment, in some kind of misguided attempt to show Mom that I was all business, and then regretted it every day of the four-month trip from Earth. I should have brought a stack of luggage taller than me—at a minimum, some decent bedding, some media gear worth using, and rations that actually qualified as food.

Seriously, I skipped breakfast this morning on the freighter. The calories just weren't worth the suffering. I'll be at the GravesUP compound in a few hours, diving face-first into the brunch of my dreams.

"Hunter Graves," poor old Nathan repeats, staring at me like I'm about to disappear, or start sparkling, or something.

"Hunter Graves," I confirm. "Of GravesUP Industries, on my way to join my family. I'll really owe you one if you can get me down to Pax today."

"Yes, of course, Mr. Graves. No problem at all," he replies, trying to . . . stand to attention, I think? "Why don't you get yourself settled on the shuttle, and I'll get the paperwork figured out for you. When you arrive, just tell the port crew you need a message transmitted to your compound, and they'll get that done for you."

"Nathan, you're the best."

Slipping past him, I stride onto the waiting shuttle, stow my bag, and sink down into the last remaining chair. The shuttle's crowded, mostly with folks in United Nations jumpsuits, and it smells like ozone and feet. *Seriously, get me to my family compound. I have seen the real world, and it's a red-hot no from me.*

It's strange, walking into an unknown crowd like this with zero security—feels like I left the house in just my underwear—but nobody seems to pay me any special attention.

As I pull on my shoulder straps, I can see the red planet below through the viewport. The ground's rough, the gleam of the sun just gilding the horizon as it starts to rise. Huge craters look like little polka dots, and mountain ranges are flattened by distance.

This is home sweet home for the next while—assuming Mom doesn't sling me back up into orbit and onto the first ship heading for Earth. I'm sure it'll be my twin sister's first suggestion.

Despite everything that's coming, I feel an unexpected tug toward the planet below. From Earth this place is nothing more than a red star, but up close it's so solid, so real.

Hey there, Mars. This should be fun.

2.

CLEO

7 HOURS, 55 MINUTES REMAINING

BREAKFAST IS THE BEST time of day to hustle people—they're still sleepy.

I scan the Pax cafeteria for a target, and zero in on a woman who's trying to carry a breakfast tray in one hand and a kid in the other while herding an extra kid through the busy morning crowd with a bump of her hip.

"Let me take that for you," I say, swooping in and relieving her of the tray before she has a chance to protest. "There are some tables on the other side of the hall there, we'll get you settled."

She glances at me for a moment, but she doesn't care that she doesn't recognize me. The usual population of the United Nations Mars base is about fifteen hundred people, but at least a third of that turns over weekly, as people head out to national or corporate compounds or return from duty. That's what's helped me stay anonymous in the three months since I got here.

It's no effort to let the crowd part me from my target, and a moment later I'm twisting away with her breakfast tray, ducking behind a couple of Martian-tall engineers and on my way to freedom.

But, Cleo, I hear you ask. *Why don't you just grab one of those yummy, yummy muffins yourself? Why did you steal that poor woman's breakfast? The line's really not that long!*

Well, to get breakfast, I'd need a registered handprint. And to get my handprint registered, I'd need to be a legal resident of Mars. And that's where we run into a problem.

I hitched a lift in on the sly and scammed my way down to Pax, but getting to a larger station is proving a lot harder than I anticipated. More often than not I'm hungry, and every minute of every day is spent figuring out how to blend in—because if I'm caught, I'll be deported quicker than you can say *Cleo has not-so-nice friends waiting for her back on Earth*. The life of a hitcher isn't all I hoped for, to be perfectly honest.

By this point, I know my way around Pax better than most of the residents, partly because I hide out in places they'd never go. I have to be creative, because every centimeter of space here is precious. Most of Pax Station is underground. If you flew over the top of us, the solar arrays would be most of what gave us away—big black panels angled toward the distant sun. This place is all about efficiency—nothing like the chaotic Jerhattan neighborhoods I grew up in.

Lucky for me, though, the hustles aren't that different, and the people here are the kind of easy marks I could have taken before I learned to read.

I scoot through the crowd and try not to reflect on the fact that, for all the people here who are pretty scammable, I'm not really coming out on top.

Still, right now I'm cruising out the cafeteria door, and taking a left to head toward water reclamation and the hydrogen plant. I've got muffins to spare, so not everything's terrible. I'll hole up somewhere in storage to eat them, and then I'll go check the transport bays. Optimism comes easier on a full belly.

Maybe today's the day I'll find a way onto a transport to one of the really big settlements, where an easier life awaits.

Maybe today's my lucky day, just waiting to begin.

3.

HUNTER

7 HOURS, 43 MINUTES REMAINING

THE ARRIVALS PORT AT Pax is almost depressing enough to make me feel bad about choking off the United Nations' funding.

I knew they were struggling, but right now I am taking in the grand vista of—and I really could not make this shit up—literally just *a room with a desk in it*. If I thought Nathan was underwhelming, I should have saved some *what the hell?* for later.

There's a patch on the wall that looks like it's sealed with duct tape.

I haven't been to the GravesUP compound in person yet, but I've seen plenty of vid, and my family's turf is . . . not like this. It's all gleaming metal and sleek white lines. There's a waterfall two stories high in our lobby, with green vines spilling down either side of it to where red and yellow flowers—our company colors—pool at the base of a fountain. Beyond that, a two-story window takes in the incredible vista of Arcadia Planitia, rusty plains stretching away into the distance.

This place, on the other hand, is all shabby, no chic—buried underground for cheaper radiation shielding, and apparently held together with spit and good luck.

Thing is, though the flowers at our base might say otherwise, the reality is that every margin here on Mars is razor-thin, and the UN has never made a real case for being here. They're a world of *no* in a place that needs to be about *yes*.

Mostly they come off like a tired parent who's going to turn this planet around this minute if these kids—these countries, these corporations—don't quit pulling their sister's hair. Except none of the kids are listening.

The locals who came down from Orbital on my shuttle stream past me without a backward glance, disappearing through the door. And then it's just me and a nervous-looking woman at a compstation.

"Mr. Graves," she says, with something vaguely related to a bow. "My colleague sent a message ahead of you. I'm all ready to get you logged in to our system and assigned to a room overnight, I just need a handprint from you."

"Overnight?" I shake my head. "I was really hoping to message for a lift over to Graves right away. They'll send a rover—I assume you guys don't have one to spare."

She grimaces apologetically. "I'm afraid the dust storm's rolling in pretty fast. It'll probably be a day or two before it clears enough to drive as far as Graves. I've put you in 39 alpha. It's roomy, as these things go."

I mentally bid farewell to the bath I've been dreaming of ever since I set foot on the freighter. I could be wrong, but I'm guessing room 39 alpha doesn't have access to spa services. "Thanks," I say, "but—"

The blare of a siren cuts me off, and we both freeze in place as a calm voice broadcasts in English.

Attention, all personnel. This is not a drill. Life-support contamination detected. Total evacuation must be complete in ten minutes. Report immediately to your assigned station. Repeat: This is not a drill.

The voice starts the announcement again, this time in Arabic, but neither of us waits to hear it.

"This way!" she shouts. I'm right on her heels as she books it out the door, swinging around to the left.

The hallways are immediately full of people rushing in the same direction, and I'm caught up in a river of humanity—folks with kids in their arms, with whatever they could grab clutched to their chests.

I'm like a baby giraffe, legs sliding out from under me as the lighter gravity hits, and every movement is overkill. I nearly go sprawling when I try to grab at the wall for support.

The loudspeaker is up to Chinese as I reach the start of the evac section. All around me, people are disappearing through doors that slide shut behind them. Through the viewport windows I can see garage doors opening so all-terrain vehicles can roar off across the Martian landscape, sending up clouds of red dust into air already heavy with it.

I feel like I'm at school again, and it's time to grab a partner.

Except nobody wants to grab me, because what if they screw up and piss me off? So everyone's paired up and I'm standing here on my own.

I pick a door at random, stumbling through into a garage that holds a six-person ATV. Five heavily padded seats are already occupied, and I pull off my backpack, shoving it under my seat as I reach for my straps.

"What are you doing here?" It's the boy in the next seat, straining forward in his harness so he can catch a glimpse of me.

"Evacuating," I reply, with a healthy dose of *what the hell do you think I'm doing?* in my tone.

"Who's that?" comes from a seat in front of us—it's a woman, her voice high with anxiety. "Is that Patrick?"

"No, can we do introductions later?" I do *not* have time for the whole Hunter Graves routine right now—none of us do.

"That's Patrick's seat!" she replies, and now everyone else around me is joining in on her protest.

I blink at her, heart still pounding, thoughts scattered, no matter how hard I reach for calm. "Is this homeroom? Are we saving seats now?"

"They're assigned," the boy beside me insists, halfway to unbuckling himself. "Are you new? This isn't your pod."

"I'm here!" calls someone from behind me, and I spin around to find myself face-to-face with . . . Patrick, I'm guessing. His brown eyes widen. "Who are you?"

I don't have time for this.

I shoulder my bag again and sling myself out of the vehicle to push past him. The door seals behind me with a hum, and once more I'm in the rush of humanity, though it's thinning out now.

I grab at a tall woman as she rushes by—she tries to shake my hand off, but when I tighten my grip to steel, she swings around.

"Where do visitors go?" I shout, raising my voice over the low thuds and clunks of the external garage doors opening and rovers abandoning the station.

"What?" She tries to pull free again.

"I just arrived. Where do I strap in?"

"Other side," she replies. "Other side of the ring. I'd run, if I were you."

I let her go, turning to sprint back the way I came, forcing my way upstream against the mass of bodies passing me.

Why the hell are the visitor pods so far away?

I can answer my own question: because the permanent population grew, and nobody had planned ahead for the inconvenient extras. They're stashed out of the way. That's what people do with unwelcome extras. Trust me on that.

And so I'm running for my life toward the extra, tacked-on pods—the afterthoughts.

It's getting quieter and quieter as I tear around the long, curved hallway that makes up the outer ring of Pax.

I've never run faster—finally, the lighter gravity works in my favor—but I could be alone in the station, my heart slamming against my ribs, my breath ragged, and now my ringing footsteps are the only sound.

The loudspeaker begins again, starting its list of announcements with English first.

Two minutes remaining. Two minutes until complete evacuation.

Does she modify the announcement by the time she makes it to the end of the list? I assume she's doing all six official languages of the United Nations. Will it be one minute remaining by the time she does it in Spanish?

Why am I thinking about that right now?

Because I don't want to think about what's actually happening.

At last, a set of double doors with VISITING PERSONNEL: EMERGENCY ATVS stenciled above.

I throw myself at one of the doors, yanking at the handle—locked.

I push off it to the second, twisting the handle so hard that a lance of pain runs from my wrist to my elbow when it refuses to turn.

"What?" My own voice surprises me. "What? You can't—"

But as I stare through the viewport window at the open garage door—at the red rocks beyond, and the rover winding its way through them—I realize they can.

And they have.

. . .

This can't be happening.

And that's when I hear the woman who greeted me, her words floating up in my memory. *I'm all ready to get you logged in to our system . . .*

But she didn't do it—she needed my handprint. The other visitors didn't even know I was here. They didn't know to wait for me.

Evacuation complete, says the voice through the loudspeaker. *Venting will commence shortly.*

"I'm here!" I shout, spinning around to shout up at the nearest speaker. "I'm here, you stupid computer!"

Evacuation complete, she repeats. *Venting will commence shortly.*

"Who are you even talking to?" I yell, hearing my voice break. "You literally just said nobody's here!" My throat's tightening, my heart trying to shove its way up from my chest. A strange part of me wants to burst out laughing.

Because somebody *is* here. I'm here. The number of times I've had this exact argument with my mother—she and this recorded announcement would really get along.

What will she think when she figures out what happened? What will my sister, Marguerite, think? Will she grieve, even for a minute?

Life support is gone. Soon—and though I've never wished in all my life that I didn't know the rules and regulations, ignorance would be bliss right now—this place will vent until it's nothing but a vacuum, removing any airborne toxins, and with them, any air left for me to breathe.

And by the time anyone realizes I was here at all—let alone that I didn't make it out—it'll be too late.

4.

CLEO

7 HOURS, 29 MINUTES REMAINING

I NEARLY JUMP OUT of my skin when the ragged voice blasts over my headset.

Mayday, mayday. This is Pax Station broadcasting a mayday on all frequencies. The evacuation is incomplete! Orbital Station, please respond!

What the *hell*?

I'm hunkered down in my storage-space hideout, jammed into a stolen pressure suit, preparing to ride out the venting procedure.

Wondering why I did not proceed quickly but calmly to my assigned evacuation vehicle, secure my straps, and depart this hot mess of a station? I mean, soon there'll be no breathable air. Not a fun place to be.

Nah. I think you're smarter than that, imaginary friend. You've figured it out: Just like the breakfast situation, they only assign you a place if they know you're here. Which is why the first thing I did on arrival was plan for this exact moment.

Because if there's one thing I know for sure, it's that if my luck can find a way to disappear down the drain when I need it most, that's exactly what it'll do. And nobody else will look out for me, that's for sure.

Mayday, mayday! the guy on the radio begins again, before sliding into . . . Arabic, I think. Presumably he's repeating the message. *Help! You left me behind! Don't take my air away!*

I shove my emergency O_2 tank up against the wall, ducking down to check the gauge one more time. I've got emergency ration packs stashed around the station, each with a fresh bundle of clothes—scruffy clothes are what'll let you down nine times out of ten—but I only have two tanks.

My plan is to ride out the initial vent in my suit, as they flush out whatever toxin has set off the alarms, and then make my way over to the other tank and haul it back here. Shouldn't be more than a day until the place manufactures enough oxygen for the general populace to come strolling back on in.

Actually, maybe this is my chance to do a little shopping. While the cats are away, this mouse could play . . .

Damn it, respond! The guy on the radio is splitting to pieces now. *You need to get hold of someone who can override the venting procedure!*

My friend, these are not very inspiring last words. I doubt Orbital's hearing them anyway through this dust storm, but—

This is Hunter Graves of GravesUP Industries! Someone respond!

Did he just say . . . ? Now *that*, on the other hand, is

compelling. What the hell is a prince like him doing in a hole like this?

Before I have time to think about it, I'm grabbing for my tank and rising to my feet. If there's even a chance he's telling the truth about who he is, I have to hurry.

Saving a billionaire could be life-changing.

I mean for him too, I guess.

But mostly for me.

5.

HUNTER

7 HOURS, 26 MINUTES REMAINING

IT'S SILENT AS DEATH in the command room. And unless someone answers my mayday, soon that'll be literal.

This *cannot* be the way I end.

Was it this quiet before? Is this the silence that comes from machinery shutting down, or is it just that I'm alone? Is the venting about to begin?

I'm standing in the center of what they call the bridge, even though this isn't a ship. It's a big, circular space with banks of desks ringing the station commander's place in the middle.

That's where I'm busy shouting into a transmitter for help that isn't coming.

The desk is so weirdly frozen in time, like the commander just stepped out for a moment, and she'll be back through the door any second now; half a toasted sandwich still sits on a plate, and the free space around her compstation is decorated with little projectors broadcasting pics and vids of her kids. There's a Tokyo Disney snow globe sitting beside a tiny plant in a painted pot.

What I care about, though, is the emergency broadcast system—and I flip back the protective case to try another mayday. My heart is still thumping so loud in my chest that I can . . .

. . . No, wait.

That's not my heart, that's *footsteps*.

I whirl around just as someone—a girl, I think—in a bulky EVA pressure suit comes hurtling through the door. She has an oxygen tank gripped in one hand instead of strapped to her back, and it swings with momentum when she pulls up short.

"What are you doing here?" The words are out before I have time to choose them, and she immediately fixes me with a look that tells me it was just as stupid a question as I think it was.

"You want to talk, or live?" she snaps—and that's when I realize her suit isn't bulky. She has a *second* suit slung over her shoulder.

"Live." I dump my backpack and practically vault the commander's desk on my way to her. She's already opening up the suit, ready to start helping me into it.

As I get closer, I can see her better inside her helmet. She has vividly red hair pulled back into a rough knot, the same rich color as the surface of the planet outside. A lock of it's falling into her big dark brown eyes. They stand out against her pale skin, the only softness about her.

Everything else, from the firm line of her mouth to the set

of her shoulders, screams businesslike competence. She moves gracefully in the low gravity, but she's short enough that she's clearly Earthborn, not Martian.

The part of my brain that regularly gets me into trouble registers that she's exactly my type, from her looks to her attitude. Except for the bit where she thinks I'm an idiot.

"Strip. Down to your underwear," she instructs me, her voice broadcast through a little speaker set into the base of her helmet. "Those clothes are too bulky to fit under a suit."

I don't even make a joke. That's how much I don't want to die. I just haul off my shirt as I hustle the last few steps toward her. I hop on first one foot and then the other as I pull off my boots, dropping them to the ground with twin thumps. The lighter Martian gravity sends me off-balance, and I grab at a desk to stay upright.

"Everything *but* your underwear," she says, underlining the words, her dark eyes daring me to get smart with her. This girl has edges so sharp, I could cut myself on them. Honestly, it's kind of hot. "The suit's Martian-sized, it's for someone leaner than you."

I unfasten my belt and drop my trousers, then step out of them. She crouches and holds the suit ready for me to step into one leg at a time, turning her head and absolutely refusing to look at anything below the belt, which, fair—we just met fifteen seconds ago.

"I tried a mayday," I say, as if conversation is going to make this somehow less personal. Once my feet are in, I reach down to take over, my fingers brushing hers for a moment before she understands and releases the suit. Quickly I haul it up over my thighs. It's tight, all right—everyone born on Mars is taller and slimmer, with the lighter gravity.

"I heard," she replies, straightening up.

"Nothing back, not even an acknowledgment ping. I thought that channel was meant to be continuously monitored by Orbital. I thought it was meant to go out to the nearest settlements."

"You should definitely get very mad at someone about that later," she replies. "Once you're in the suit, we have to get an O_2 tank and hook you up."

"Hurry up, in other words."

"Hey, not so stupid after all. You keep getting the suit sealed, I'll try my luck with the mayday. Is there anything they can do, though, even if they do receive a transmission?"

"They can override the venting procedure."

"Who can? The UN can override any system on Mars, but who can override the UN? Doesn't that kind of miss the point of what they're here for, if someone else can control them?"

"There are UN staff on Orbital. They can help us remotely. If they know we're here."

She nods, and weaves her way through the rings of desks as I wrestle the suit over my hips and then jump up and down on the spot to try to coax it higher at the crotch. And yeah, I wait until her back's turned for that bit of ridiculousness.

There was no need for me to bother, though—she's not paying any attention to me.

"I was just using the emergency channel. I couldn't get the

commander's station to power up without her handprint," I call out, about two seconds before she hefts the Disney snow globe in one hand and then uses the edge of its base to smash open the casing around the display monitor.

Then, as I watch open-mouthed, she pulls off her gloves and flexes her fingers. Next she yanks out two wires and . . . hot-wires the station? The screen flickers to life, flickers again, and then I'm staring at the commander's welcome screen.

"How did . . . ?"

She looks up, guarded. "I'm an engineering student. Any chance we can access the shutdown controls from here? The commander didn't stop to log out before she left, so we have her authority, but I don't know where to start looking. Why aren't you getting your suit on?"

I've only got the suit up waist-high—it really is too small, and the second I get my arms into it, I don't think I'm even going to be able to bend them. So I tie the arms around my waist for now as I jog over to join her. "I know my way around the system."

"You know how to impersonate the Pax Station commander?" She sounds skeptical. "Are you sure? Should I put my gloves back on and seal my suit before you try this?"

"This system wasn't built for Pax—it's a mod of the GravesUP systems. Ours was the first compound on Mars. Everyone uses a version of our software. Why reinvent it when you can't do any better?" I glance sideways at her, and she still doesn't look convinced. "I'm Hunter Graves," I add.

She rolls her eyes. "Yeah, I caught that when you were

squawking over the PA system." To underline the point, she flails her arms around in what I assume is an unflattering impression of me during that broadcast.

Huh. Mocking isn't usually how this goes. Usually, there's a fairly predictable response, and though I don't enjoy it, I'm used to it. First the eyes widen slightly, then the lips part as if the person meeting me has seen the kind of dessert that makes you want to eat it all and lick the spoon. Meanwhile, their internal algorithms start to run frantically as they try to figure out how they can make the most of being this close to the actual Hunter Graves.

Not this girl, though. Then again, she's an engineering student on a crappy station. I'm guessing schmoozing isn't her thing.

So I flip her off, which at least stops the Muppet impression she's doing, and we turn to study the opening screen shoulder to shoulder, the smooth fabric of her suit pressing against my arm.

"Do you have a name?" I try.

"Cleo," she replies, leaning in to stare at the screen. "So can you navigate this?"

"The menus look pretty similar. One way to find out."

I tap the slender cuff at my wrist to bring it to life, and swipe one hand toward the commander's station, telling it to find a way in and connect. In the time it takes me to draw a breath, it does.

Quickly I lift a hand, throwing a larger version of the screen up in front of us, bright lines projected into the air. I use both my hands to split it into two, and swipe through, running two searches at once. Text and images go flying past, offering me access to all the different corners of the station. I glide through them, not letting my mind hitch on any one thing, instead absorbing the flow, letting it wash over me.

I've been doing this since I was a kid—this kind of system is the earliest playground I remember—and there's something almost relaxing about sinking into it. I know what I'm doing here. I'm in control.

I plunge deeper to find comms and life support—not out in the open where they'd be easy to mess with—and suddenly I find the process menus I'm looking for.

And that's when I screech to a halt. And I blink. And then I grab at the virtual screen with both hands to zoom in on the section I want, fumbling as I try to move too quickly.

"What did you find?" Cleo smacks me in the bicep to get my attention.

"It's . . . this can't be right."

"What can't?"

I reload the displays, as though they'll say something new this time.

"Hunter." Cleo's voice is a warning. "It would be such a pity if I had to kill you, after finding a suit to save you with and all."

I give my head a shake. "The system is broadcasting all the emergency evacuation messages it's supposed to. It's running the alarms, making the announcements."

"We know this," Cleo points out.

"But Cleo, there's no prep underway to *actually vent the station*. It should be equalizing air pressure, it should—"

Cleo breaks in before I get too far down the list. "Are you saying it's making the noise, but not doing the thing?"

I frown. "Sure looks that way."

She peers at the list of unexecuted commands, though I don't think she understands them. "I mean . . . that's good, right? Does that mean the station's not about to vent all our breathable air?"

"Doesn't seem so."

"What about the toxin that caused this? Where's that? Are we in danger from it?"

"I can't see any evidence it even exists."

"Huh." She's frowning at the screen too now. "Also good, I guess?"

"I mean, better than the alternative, that's for sure. But mostly what it is, is really, *really* weird."

6.

CLEO

7 HOURS, 21 MINUTES REMAINING

If I'm being perfectly honest, Hunter Graves is mighty fine. I did not expect this to be the case.

I've never laid eyes on him before—they make sure of that—but I've thought about him plenty of times.

I thought he'd be some kind of inbred aristocrat with a weak chin. Instead, he's standing beside me, bare-chested, and my oh my, someone has been doing his exercises on the trip.

I've always enjoyed imagining him in a sweeping black cloak, all the better to be evil in, but right now he looks like an action figure whose shirt fell off. I've gotten used to lean Martian bodies in the three months I've been here, but Hunter is clearly planning on making the return journey to Earth—he's been keeping his strength up, in readiness for the higher gravity back home.

He's got olive-brown skin, tousled dark brown hair, full lips, and the kind of bearing and posture that screams money. He's also got—I may have mentioned this already—no shirt on. There are entirely too many abs on display. Yum.

It's a pity he's a filthy rich capitalist whose family exploits the poor every morning before breakfast. Ask me how I know. Or don't. We don't have time for a story that long.

For now, though I'd like to kick him in the tender parts just for possessing Graves DNA, I keep it nice. Because if he owes me one—for saving his life, for instance—I'll be able to write my own ticket to anywhere on Mars. His family has that kind of pull. And I'm going to need that ticket when the base crew returns and starts asking who I am.

Back on Earth, the Graves family have their claws in almost every part of life in one way or another. Their logo is on the food I eat. Both my local malls are GravesUP branded. They run the media, have major stakes in health care; they probably made my underwear. It's bad enough that you can't turn around without seeing something they control. For me, that greed took a personal toll.

Pretending I'm happy to breathe the same air as one of them is unpleasant, but I can do it if it'll get me where I need to go. Which is anywhere but here.

"All right," I try, dragging my mind back to the problem of my immediate survival. "What do you think they're seeing up on Orbital? Will they know when the station doesn't vent?"

"Great question." He gets a line between his eyebrows when

he concentrates. "I don't know why it's doing this, so I'm not sure what it's going to broadcast to them. They won't get a visual, because the dust storm's completely surrounded us by now. And there's no way to know if they're receiving any status updates, given I couldn't even ping them with the mayday."

"So if they think we're dead, we could be here awhile," I conclude. "Hey, technically the base is abandoned now, right? That means we could claim the territory, doesn't it?"

He huffs a soft laugh. "Almost. You're on staff here, though. So actually, you're all that's standing between the great United Nations and the rest of Mars. Whatever they're paying you, you should ask for a raise."

Whoops. Yes, right, on staff here at Pax. That's definitely me. Engineering student, that's what I said. Shut up, Cleo.

"I want to see if I can get a signal out. I can try—" He pauses as his attention is dragged back to the data stream in front of him, and the silence draws out. I don't know what he's doing to that system, but he's romancing it hard—I guess having a way with technology is in his blood.

It's nearly a minute later—I spend the time contemplating his profile, which is irritatingly flawless—when his shoulders drop and he lets out a slow breath of pure relief, tipping his head back to gaze up at the ceiling.

"Are we smiling now?" I prompt him, though I don't smack him in the arm again, because that was a lot of skin last time, and my gloves are still off.

"Cleo, I think our luck just turned around." He points to a

tiny schematic in the corner of one of his screens, enlarging it with a quick gesture. "Airlock sixteen just opened. I think the base crew's coming back."

He looks across at me with a grin that's blindingly charming, but somewhere in the back of my mind, something's shifting uneasily. As he studies my face, his smile slowly starts to die away.

"Why that airlock?" I say softly, in answer to the question in his green eyes. "All the ground evac vehicles took off to the west. Sixteen is on the *east* side. Why would someone circle all the way around to the other side to let themselves back in? It's not even a major entry point."

Before he can reply, a voice rings out in the distance. It's a man's, rough and too loud. "Honey, I'm home!"

Hunter and I both go still at once. Then he speaks quietly. "That's a weird thing to say in an emergency situation, don't you think?"

There's a prickling on the back of my neck that usually means someone I'm running from has spotted me. I totally agree it's a weird thing for someone to yell right now, but I'm trying to play the engineering student, not the career criminal who always suspects she's about to get screwed. "I guess? Maybe they know it's not an emergency? He must have his helmet off, if we can hear him at this distance."

But when our eyes meet, I'm surprised to see that Hunter looks as wary as I feel. Living a life like his, I wouldn't have thought he'd know how to be cautious.

"I've had a lot of training," he says slowly. "Because I'd make a high-value hostage. And one of the things they're always telling me is that I should listen to my gut. Listen when that twitch between my shoulder blades tells me I'm not safe."

"I learned that . . . in a different place," I say, one part of my brain wondering what he'd make of the back alleys where I found my danger. Wondering what he'd say if I told him who put me in that danger, without ever knowing or caring. "But yeah, I hear you."

"Let's step back out of sight. If we're wrong, we can come strolling out and hug them one by one until they beg for mercy, no harm done. We don't even have to admit we were lurking."

My heart's starting to speed up. I nod. Because that spot between *my* shoulder blades? It's twitching too.

With a gesture he dismisses the screens, and I brush the broken plastic cover for the monitors onto the ground and set the snow globe back in place.

Hunter scoops up his bag and retrieves my gloves for me, and I dart off to grab the boots and trousers he dumped on the floor. Then we hurry through the main entrance to the north.

I flick off the hallway lights at the control panel, and we press in against the wall, standing together in the darkness and silence. I'm nearer the door, Hunter just beyond me. I wish now that he'd put his damn shirt back on, but I don't want to tell him I've noticed he's not wearing one.

"This is probably for nothing," he whispers. "I'm sure there's a reason they've come in this way. He even said he's home."

"And yet both our creep monitors went off at the same time," I point out.

"Right. If there's even a chance they're hitchers or some sort of criminals, we can't trust them. They could do anything. You know what those people are like."

I think I make a sound, and my breath leaves me like a punch.

That's me he's talking about so casually. *I'm* one of the hitchers he can't trust—one of the people his family would prefer to leave behind, while they build themselves a new world on Mars, screwing the old one in the process.

How the hell am I going to convince this guy to give me a ride out of here once he works out who—and what—I am?

Then footsteps sound across the room, and four figures in pressure suits come stalking in, fanning out to different workstations as if they know exactly where they're going.

There are no Pax markings on what they're wearing—could they be from another station, come to investigate the evacuation alarm? Their helmets are already off, though, so they're clearly not worried about asphyxiating when the station vents.

They take up their places—all unsmiling, all business. There's an efficiency to their movements that has me holding my breath, as if they're predators and might hear me exhale.

The leader—I swear, I know by the way he walks—stalks over to the commander's station. He's in maybe his forties, his head shaved down to dark stubble, built like he could fight three guys at once. He wears a patch over his left eye, which has to be a choice given how easy a bionic would be to fit. The patch should make him look like a fake pirate, but actually just makes him look like he could rip you in two and not break his stride. Everything about him screams single-minded purpose.

The Pirate sweeps everything off the desk in one quick,

sharp gesture. The snow globe smashes, sending up fragments of glass and drops of water. The plant's pot shatters, dirt scattering across the floor. Then he sets down a portable system on the desk and starts plugging it into the commander's outlets.

"Minute one begins on my mark," he says, and each of the invaders raises a hand to check their wrist unit. "We have seven hours and fifteen minutes. Mark."

7 HOURS, 15 MINUTES REMAINING

Two of the others start peeling off their pressure suits, ready to get comfortable, but one woman puts down the crate she's carrying and throws open the lid. She moves with the kind of deadly grace that a snake uses to hypnotize small animals right before it lashes out at them.

She pulls out a pistol and tosses it to the nearest woman.

Her teammate catches it, turns it over in her hands like she knows exactly how to use it, and then secures it at her waist. And then she turns around, and I catch sight of her face. She has a hard expression and a tattoo that runs straight across her forehead like a tiara, brightly colored jewels drawn around a silver band that seems almost to shine.

Shit.

I know this woman. She usually runs with the Gramercy gangs, and I last saw her back on Earth.

In an instant I'm back in an alleyway, my lungs burning, my legs giving out as I push myself to keep running, keep running, *keep running*. I know I can't, I know it's impossible—and I know that if she catches me, if they catch me, they'll leave me bleeding on the concrete, an example for others. An example for my mother, who'll never even know, though they don't believe that.

I feel the rough plasteel of the apartment building's wall as I grab at its corner, swing myself around into an intersection, and dive behind a snack cart. The vendor looks down, and I see him weigh it up.

He hides me, and they'll trash his stuff if they figure it out. He gives me up, and he has to watch what happens next.

I see the moment I become invisible to him, as his gaze slides away and he hails the next buyer. I curl into a ball, hugging myself, trying to keep my breathing quiet.

Here and now, my breath seems to freeze in my throat, and I'm straight into another memory.

I'm in a club, looking for someone to hustle, the music pumping through my veins, sweat sticking to my skin as bodies writhe around me. I push through the crowd and come face to face with her—*Sabrina Barr*—her tattooed gems picked out with crystals for the night, her usual fatigues switched out for a sheath dress.

I freeze as her hand comes up to steady herself. Our eyes lock. I see the moment she makes me, recognition clicking into place.

My hands come up too, ready to shove her away backward, to twist and plunge onto the dance floor. But she grabs my wrist, her hand closing around it like a vise.

"Easy," she says, raising her voice above the thumping bass.

And then, impossibly, she winks. "I'm not on the clock right now. I'm only an asshole for money."

And then she releases me and turns away, and I'm left dry-mouthed and shaking, cradling my wrist as if it's been burned.

Sabrina's not a terrible human, but when she's paid to do a job, she does it. In my experience, Sabrina doesn't do nice jobs. If she's here, this is . . . yeah. Not a good time to be here too.

I turn my head toward Hunter, and his gaze is waiting for me, eyes huge. He might not see any familiar faces, but he's obviously figured out the same thing I have.

Whatever the next seven hours and fifteen minutes hold, it's going to be bad, bad news.

7.

HUNTER

7 HOURS, 13 MINUTES REMAINING

I FOLLOW CLEO DOWN the hallway and around a corner, my breath coming too fast, sweat prickling the back of my neck.

Glancing over her shoulder, she shoves her fingertips into the seal between two sliding doors and, with a soft grunt of effort, levers them open. I slide my own hands in to help her, and together we keep them apart long enough to slip through before they close behind us.

We're in . . . is this living quarters? It can't be; it's smaller than the room I had on the ship out from Earth. I could cross this whole space in three long strides, and there are *four* bunks in here.

Just like the commander's desk, this place was abandoned on a moment's notice. Beds are unmade, and a kid's remote-controlled toy rover lies in the middle of the floor. And none of that matters, because we just saw a bunch of criminals take over the station. Why am I looking at toys?

"What the hell?" I whisper. "What the *hell*? Who are those people?"

Cleo shakes her head, leaning back against the closed doors like she wants to block them with her body. She's rattled, lips parting as she reaches for words—then she presses them tightly together again and shakes her head once more.

She's an engineering student. This must be so, so far from her world. I mean, it's not like I hang around with criminals all day—or at least, people keep it to white-collar crime in my circles—but the idea of a threat isn't new to me.

I should try to comfort her so she doesn't shut down—it'll be even harder to get us out of this if she freaks out. But what can I say that won't sound like I'm delusional? It's definitely *not* going to be okay.

Still, I came out here to show my mother that I could do this—that I could lead.

"Okay." I'm surprised how steady my voice sounds. "The first thing is to try and let someone know we're alive in here. Carefully, in case our new friends are monitoring comms." I spin around to find the inhabitants' personal console, set into the wall. "Can you hot-wire this one too?"

"Probably easier than out there," Cleo says, crossing over to inspect it. "Lower security." She takes her gloves from me and shoves them into her belt, hesitates, then unseals her helmet and sets it down beside her. Then she starts to unzip her suit. "Safe to do this, I guess, if they've taken theirs off." Her voice is warmer, richer, now it's not being piped through the helmet's external mic.

She peels the suit down to her waist and ties the arms there, like I've done. She's wearing a gray tank beneath it, and her arms are covered in tattoos. Flowers and vines curl up from her wrists, twining around each other in vivid greens and purples. There are freckles across her pale shoulders, covering her skin like the sweep of the Milky Way. She's been outside in the sun, and over the long term too. So from a lower-class background, then. I wonder how the hell she got to Mars.

She produces a tool from a pocket at her hip and jams it into one of the outlets, biting her lower lip in concentration as she carefully pries it open.

Engineering is physical work, I guess—she's lean and strong, and I catch myself studying her face, where her red hair's escaping the knot at the back of her neck to curl around her cheekbones.

Hunter, no. Absolutely not. For a start, this is a life-threatening situation, and she's probably terrified and counting on you to—

"Okay, got it," she says, straightening, and I realize the display's lit up. "Your turn."

"Hey, look at us," I manage, snapping back to reality. "Already a team."

Cleo fixes me with a look and pretends to wave a cheerleader's pom-poms in the air. Attitude is better than fear, though, so I let her have it.

I haul over a crate to use as a chair and link my cuff to the console, then trigger the virtual keyboard commands. Some things are easier to do the old-fashioned way, and I want to tiptoe *very* carefully through the electronic landscape just now.

Cleo watches me for a moment, then, apparently satisfied I'm doing what I'm supposed to, she turns away. Out of the corner of my eye I can see her quietly turning over the place, going through piles of possessions with a quick efficiency.

I speak softly, partly to distract myself from the bunch of potential murderers a few rooms over, and partly to distract her. "Looks like a family lives here, I guess. Did you come out here with yours?"

"No, I'm on my own," she replies, just as quiet, in a tone that doesn't invite a follow-up question. "Your mother's at your family compound, though, isn't she? I saw her on the news. And your sister?"

"Sure are," I agree. "Unfortunately, they have no idea *I'm* here." And if they did, my sister at least would laugh herself sick. My mother would fold her arms and wait for me to prove myself.

"What, they think you're still up on Orbital?" Cleo asks, peering inside a storage box.

I hesitate, but now isn't the time to get into a conversation about the fact that my remaining family thinks I'm still on Earth. And anyway, why would I explain that to a girl I don't even know?

"I didn't get logged in here before the alarm went off," I say, which is true, if incomplete.

She snorts softly and shakes her head, moving on. "I found some protein bars. I'll start a stash. If I get really lucky, I might even find you a shirt."

I look down and blink. "Huh. I think I left it on the bridge.

That was a limited-edition Mirrorball Scoundrel shirt, too. Did you hear their new album?"

She makes a noise I can't interpret, but that I think might be disapproval.

We both fall silent as I work, my fingers flying over a keyboard made of light, carefully navigating my way through the station's menus. Walking through them is like walking in my grandfather's footsteps—thirty-one years ago, he sat only a few hours away from here by rover, wrestling with these same menus inside a small domed encampment. The first man on Mars—the genius who gave us the red star.

This planet is his resting place. It won't be mine.

"So," I say eventually, trying and failing to fight off a sinking feeling. "You want the bad news, or the worse news?"

Cleo sighs and sits on the edge of one of the bunks. "Warm me up slowly. Give me the bad first."

I swallow. "I'm trying to get a message out to GravesUP, or any of the neighboring compounds. I know the West African Union, Ares Tech, and FreyaCo aren't far from here. Our new friends have the system ring-fenced, though—nothing's getting out, and if I try to brute-force it, they'll definitely know."

"Would you know how to do it, if it came down to it?" Cleo asks.

"I could, but they'd be able to trace it right to the terminal. They'd find us before help could possibly arrive."

"So we can't tell anyone we're here, or ask for help," she says, voice muffled as she scrubs at her face. "What's the *worse* news?"

"There is one message getting out. The station actually *is* broadcasting on the emergency channel. It's saying the venting procedure is now complete, which means—"

"That even when your people do work out you're here, they're going to think you're dead."

"Right. And nobody's going to show up here until the station tells them it's done repressurizing. Why would they risk it, when I'm a corpse? No need to rush in for a dead guy."

That's assuming Nathan even thinks to tell someone I'm here. And why would he? As far as he knows, I was registered upon arrival. Will the woman who didn't check me in say something? Probably not—she took me right to the evac garages. She'll assume I got away.

God, what a cluster.

Cleo peels her hands away from her face. "Okay, so our best bet is, what? Hole up and hide, and hope they leave at the end of their countdown?" She doesn't sound optimistic. "Keep our pressure suits near?"

"I just wish we knew what they want," I mutter, turning back to the screen, letting the enviro displays scroll idly by. "Are they trying to claim the territory, because the base is abandoned? Maybe yes—they don't know you're here. Or maybe no—they got here pretty fast to be jumping on a chance."

"Unless they created the chance," she points out. "But would anyone really make that kind of move on the United Nations?"

I shake my head slowly. "Graves sure wouldn't," I say. And I can tell that sheltered though she might be, even Cleo reads the subtext: *If* we *wouldn't do it, then nobody would.* "Maybe it's some sort of Mars For All protest?"

"What, against the UN?" She shakes her head. "They're the only ones who've even hinted Mars shouldn't be more exclusive than a country club. Why would a protest group take on their only allies?"

"Simplistic, but I see your point."

"What, then?" she murmurs. "Seven hours and fifteen minutes until what?"

"I might be able to figure that out, if I can see what they're doing with the commander's compstation."

Cleo lets out a slow breath. "I think we should find a safer base, first. We're still not that far from them, and depending on how closely they're looking, they might notice these living quarters are drawing more power than they should."

"Hey, look at you, thinking like our criminal friends." I try for a tease, but it doesn't land—she flushes, her pale skin reddening, like I hit a nerve. "I'm sorry." What's going on, am I stumbling over my words right now? "I didn't mean—"

"No, of course, you're fine." She cuts me off firmly. "I think we should head to the facilities wing. The hydrogen plant, the oxygenators, the greenhouse, the fish farms, they're all grouped together. They'd have to be drawing a lot of power, if they're still running, so nobody will notice whatever we use. And there are plenty of places to hide."

"Then let's do it," I agree. "Carefully."

8.

CLEO

7 HOURS, 7 MINUTES REMAINING

AS WE SNEAK ALONG the hallways like a couple of criminals—which I guess we are, only one of us does it in fancy, corporate ways—it's so quiet I can hear the machinery of the dome working. Usually the fans that circulate our air are drowned out by the sounds of conversation and footsteps and daily life.

"Maybe they'll see a heat signature up on Orbital," Hunter whispers. "Realize all the plant's still working, and the station's not shut down?"

"We're buried underground," I point out softly, keeping the *duh* out of my tone. "There's tons of dirt and rock shielding us."

I've heard GravesUP has their radiation shielding built into their compound walls—there are materials that'll do that for you—but the UN's always scrambling for budget, and underground is cheaper, and lasts longer. You just don't get many windows. If Hunter Graves wanted someone to monitor this place properly from Orbital, his family shouldn't have led the charge to screw the UN on funding.

"Right, I knew that," Hunter mutters. "Underground. Okay, keep thinking."

His lordship is just a step behind me, in a T-shirt that says RED STAR EXPLORATION CONFERENCE 2067 on it, stolen from whoever's quarters we just used. At least it covers him up from waist to neck, and shields me from distraction. As for the neck-up beauty, I'm going to ignore it. I have twice as much reason as him to stay focused.

He just has to survive this. I have to live through it *and* convince him to help get me off this base despite the fact that I'm everything that's wrong with the world.

Trauma bonds people, right? And this is for sure traumatic. The best I can do is stay on his good-ish side and hope—assuming we're alive seven hours from now—that this bond carries him through however he feels when he finds out how I got here.

I'm not sure it'll really make a difference that I didn't visibly roll my eyes at him when he forgot not everybody gets to be aboveground, but it's worth a try. He clearly thinks I'm helpless and naive and that he needs to rescue me. If he wants to feel like he's saving the day, that's fine. Whatever.

We make our way through silent corridors, keeping our footsteps light.

It's been eight months since I saw Sabrina, or any of the Gramercy crew. Three months here at Pax, four months crammed into the cargo hold of a freighter, and before that, one month hiding out in a basement in Jerhattan, hyperventilating about the fact that my mother left town and tagged me with all her debts on the way out.

Which, people, is why I don't know a lot about bonding.

Sabrina won't care that I owe her old bosses money. Will she? That can't be Gramercy she's with now—she's leveled up. Then again, it won't matter if she cares. She'll have to wipe me out if she sees me, as a witness to whatever they're doing here.

Or, a tiny voice whispers in the back of my mind, *maybe they'd take on an extra pair of hands? She knows you. She knows you get things done. That could be a way out of here.*

Three damn months here, trapped by the UN's meticulous recordkeeping. Hunter Graves, of all people, is the first person I've had an extended conversation with in all that time. That's probably what they mean when they say to be careful what you wish for. I wasn't *that* lonely.

I thought the hard part of my Mars trip would be blackmailing my way onto the freighter, or forcing my contact to hold his nerve long enough to get me down on his transport. I never figured *this* would be where it came unglued—that I'd end up trapped at my first port of call.

It feels like I'm jumping from lily pad to lily pad, watching each of them sink beneath the water behind me, with no idea what's ahead. Safe shores, or a dead end?

If I can just get to a bigger station—GravesUP has over twenty thousand people now, and there are others catching up fast—then I can find the local underworld, and blend in, get back to the kind of life I know how to live, hustle to hustle. Or even—though I can hardly whisper this to myself, even in the secrecy of my own mind—stop hustling? Just . . . get a job? Live?

Revealing myself to Sabrina would be a high-stakes move. She might just shoot me to eliminate a complication, and even if she didn't, it would push that whispered part of my dream farther away. And sure, it's probably a foolish, impossible thing to even let myself think. But I can't help dreaming of it anyway. This is a place where I could be something—a place where I could stop running, if only they'd let me in.

I should save turning to Sabrina for when I run out of options. And for now, I should focus on the present moment—not spiral from plan to plan, from Hunter to Sabrina and back again. Easier said than done, though.

Hunter moves up to walk beside me, and I catch him an instant before he strolls into an intersection. I grab at his arm and yank him back, then edge forward to take a look around the corner *carefully*.

Maybe Sabrina *is* a better bet than this boy.

As I get a peek at the hallway we're intersecting with, I freeze. Two new mercenaries are striding toward us. They don't look wary—why would they be?—but they have guns at their hips.

I use my grip on Hunter to drag him backward, and at least he doesn't resist. I look around wildly for somewhere to hide in the handful of seconds we've got before they turn the corner.

There's a door two steps back, and I yank it open and step into a storage closet, pulling Hunter after me. He pulls the door closed after him, and we both stand perfectly still.

We're nose to nose, bodies pressed together. He's twisting his arm around to keep the door from flying open, which only pushes him closer to me. I can feel every tiny shift, feel his muscles contract as he keeps his grip on the edge of the door.

I try to keep my breathing shallow, so I don't press against him any more than I have to, but the warmth of his skin bleeds through our thin shirts as his eyes meet mine.

His face is cut in half by the sliver of light that comes through the crack in the doorjamb, and I take in the hint of stubble at his jaw, the smooth lines of his cheekbones. I thought his eyes were all green, but now I can see they're flecked with a golden brown.

Footsteps pass us by, and I catch a snatch of conversation. "Oh, it'll be structural. A blast that big? Guaranteed."

And then they're receding. We both let out a soft breath, but that only presses us closer together. Hunter doesn't move yet, but keeps listening, head tilted. Maybe a minute later, he eases the door open a touch and turns his head to press an eye to the gap.

We slip out silently, and we move a lot more carefully after that.

"Only a few more blocks over," I whisper, barely audible, and he nods. We're following the ring corridor, a long hallway that circles the base. The ceiling is a curved dome cut into the dirt and rock, and lights are fixed every ten meters or so, powered by the huge solar arrays above us. They can't be doing much business in the middle of a dust storm, but the lights are bright enough for now.

I don't breathe properly until I see the door marked GREENHOUSE.

Warm, damp air greets us as we make our way inside.

Around us, sunlamps hang from the ceiling, and plants burst from their shelves, filling every available centimeter of space. The air itself is practically green, and everything's so *alive*, brushing my sleeves as I pass by, as if each and every leaf wants to say hi.

I haven't been in here since I arrived—the gardening crew is always on hand—and unexpected tears prickle my eyes. Something in my body unclenches at the sight of the greenery.

This is the only place inside the settlement where chaos reigns. You can't plan for exactly how plants will grow, after all. The greenhouse breaks the rules when nothing else can.

When I was maybe five or six, I found a little green shoot growing through a crack in the concrete by our front door. It was the first plant I'd ever seen outside the ones in glass cases in shopping malls, all carefully pruned and controlled.

This little guy was just pushing up a green stalk and three tiny leaves, and it seemed like magic. I got a plastic quickmeal pack and cut it up so I could build a little fort around it, and dripped water onto it each morning.

It lasted until it was stupid enough to try to grow a flower. Then someone pulled it out by the roots and took it for themselves. I don't really know what else I was expecting.

"That's the way the world goes," my mother told me.

When I got older, I got those green shoots and that purple flower tattooed up my arms, as a reminder that there's always a way to survive, even if you have to force yourself through a crack in what seems like concrete. I turned those little green shoots into a whole plant on my body, big and strong.

Here on Mars, this huge room bursting with rows of greenery feels more like another world than the red planet outside.

Originally, the plants here on Mars were for the food and O_2 recyc programs, but a lot of people come to the greenhouse just for the green. Turns out that's important to humans, even on the red planet. Maybe more so here than anywhere.

I don't know what Hunter makes of it—I can't imagine what kinds of gardens they have at the GravesUP compound, or at his home on Earth, but I bet they're spectacular. This is pretty nice too, though.

We make our way along the path until we find a table full of green shoots in little containers, and tools for digging and so on, abandoned mid-task. Someone was potting seedlings, and left them behind when the alarm went off, along with a jacket that tells me that person was about my size, and according to their name patch, called Ash House. I claim the jacket, tucking it under my arm, and check out the rest of their belongings.

"Are those cookies?" Hunter murmurs, breaking the silence that's been strung between us since we left the closet.

He sounds so hopeful. Making him fit into the villainous shape I have pre-cut for him is harder than I'd have thought.

"Put them in your bag," I say, passing them over. He's still carrying the backpack he came down from the shuttle with. He stows them, and we move deeper into our sanctuary, crossing a small footbridge over a pool of water. Silvery fish with trailing fanlike fins glide by soundlessly beneath us, with no idea they're on another planet.

"Tilapia," Hunter murmurs. And then, just as I'm trying the word out in my mouth, thinking it flows like their trailing fins: "They're a great source of protein, and it helps that they reproduce. Also, back when the trip out used to be longer, the crew found it really soothing to look at them."

"Even though they were going to eat them?"

"Humans are complicated. It was my aunt who brought the first fish to Mars, you know."

How excellent for your aunt, Hunter Graves. My aunt worked in one of your family's factories, making personal transport vehicles she couldn't afford to drive.

It's on the far side of the bridge that I see what I was really looking for—a rack of half a dozen EVA pressure suits hanging on pegs. The suits need to be tight enough to stop your body exploding all over the place in the lower pressure outside the habs. (I kid, I kid. You wouldn't explode. You'd just bleed from your eyes and then die, relax.) The one I tried to cram Hunter into is just too small, though.

I go for the largest one, holding it up against him. Thank you, Finn Crowhurst, for leaving your suit behind.

"You want me to put it on now?" Hunter asks, grimacing. "It's like running around in a wetsuit."

"You're *complaining* about a piece of lifesaving equipment?" There's more edge than I intended in my voice—though seriously, is he? I make a mental note that next time I think he's hot, all I need to do is get him to open his mouth and speak. "You don't think there's an outside chance we might need these?"

With a put-upon sigh, he starts peeling out of his too-small suit, and great, now I have Hunter Graves, billionaire and most eligible guy in the galaxy, back in his underwear. Again.

I turn around and study a frame where the locals are growing cherry tomatoes, picking one and popping it into my mouth. I press my teeth against it for a moment, feeling the pressure, and then it breaks open, and I nearly moan. I haven't tasted a tomato in *years*. Forget the boy in his underwear. I'll take food every time.

"Uh, you okay there?" Hunter asks from behind me, and I swallow my mouthful and clear my throat. Maybe I actually did moan.

"I'm fine. You can just tie your suit off around your waist, I think we should be safe here for a minute. Whatever they're after, it's probably not in a flower bed."

"I didn't like the way that guy in the hallway was talking about structural damage," he says, and I hear my own stress in his voice.

"Me neither." I close my eyes for a moment, desperately wishing I weren't going to say what I'm about to say. "And I don't want to be a downer, but . . ."

"Yeah. I don't have a long list of reasons why he'd have been talking about blasting anything."

"Right? In fact, I have deeply worrying ideas about why that was coming up in conversation."

He speaks quietly. "I think we have to ask whether they're going to destroy the place on their way out. Or at least damage it very badly. It's the easiest way to hide that they were ever here, once they've got whatever they came for. Blow up all the systems and expose everything to vacuum. Who'd even be looking for evidence, when it seems obvious what went wrong?"

I nod slowly. I know people like this, and it's what any of them would do.

"Yeah." I swallow hard. "And if we're going to figure out what their plan is—let alone how to survive it—then we can't just hunker down and hide and wait for them to leave. We need to chase information. And fast."

9.

HUNTER

6 HOURS, 57 MINUTES REMAINING

What "chasing information" looks like in reality is hunting through the nearby workstations for one whose log-in I can figure out.

I should have asked Cleo for hers before she disappeared—she's gone to scout the recycling center, where they handle water reclamation and things like that, to get the lay of the land around our new greenhouse base. She's holding it together pretty well, all things considered.

So I sit here and poke at the system, muttering to myself. The commander's station on the bridge was easy—she left it without logging out. But it's been a while now and everyone's connection here has idled, which means I need a password.

Tragically, nobody has used *password*, which is great news for the local IT techs and a pain in the ass for me.

I decide to try my luck with the bank of monitors near a wall of tomato plants and passion fruit vines—I've got a good feeling about the gardening crew. I'm betting on them being less precise than the engineers.

It's Susanna Hirano who comes through for me. Her whole station is decorated with pictures of daisies, she has a paperweight with a preserved daisy inside it that must have taken up an insane amount of her personal luggage allowance, and her password is—*come on, Susanna, we know better than this*—"Daisy123!"

I sigh out loud when the cuff shows me her password file, but I waste no time assuming Susanna's identity and getting elbows-deep in the code.

It takes less than a minute to see that I'm not the only one exploring Pax's operating systems. Our new friends are getting their hands dirty too.

My mother would be appalled to know I sneak around in the backs of systems like this as often as I do, but ironically, she's the one who forced me to learn it.

Here's a thing to know about my family: When someone goes from zero to life-alteringly rich, one of two things happens. Either the next generation figures out how to sustain it, or they blow it in spectacular style.

My mother falls into the first camp, and she's so committed to keeping GravesUP locked on target that she's locked me out.

Which is, in fact, why I'm here, in a freaking greenhouse, hacking my way into some flower-loving scientist's workstation, trying to figure out how to stop a bunch of mercenaries from killing me.

I'm just saying, if she hadn't forced me into coming to Mars without her blessing, I'd have been on a different ship, and I'd be having a very different day right now. But I'd have needed a very different childhood for that.

Growing up, my twin sister, Marguerite, and I were inseparable. In the bloody waters of corporate politics, we were two young sharks, and we loved hunting together. We talked spreadsheets and mergers at the dinner table, and hostile takeovers for dessert. We knew what it meant to be a Graves.

Still, there was one division of assets we didn't see coming: our parents' divorce, when we were thirteen.

I was out of favor at the time. My sister and I had been caught hacking into the servers of a greentech company we wanted to acquire, and I'd taken the fall for it.

Our mother's never been the cuddly sort. She's utterly focused on GravesUP, and we spent our lives in orbit around her, living and dying by her rare attention, and her rarer approval.

We both grew up understanding we were part of a legacy bigger than any one individual. Mom holds the keys to the castle—to our way into being a part of GravesUP's future. Our job has always been to convince her to let down the drawbridge.

When it came to the greentech hacking incident, she didn't mind that we found a back door into a company we wanted to acquire. At thirteen, we were old enough to go after what we wanted.

She was just mad we were stupid enough to get caught.

Looking back, I can't believe I was gullible enough to take

the hit for it. I still don't know why I did, except that Marguerite suggested it. I adored my sister, and I trusted her completely.

"Even if she locks you down for a minute, one of us will still be able to act on what we learned," she said. We were twins. We were a team—so I went along with it.

I was so, so stupid.

The divorce happened shortly after that. Mom left the family compound and took Marguerite with her. At the time, I thought I wasn't going too because I was still in trouble.

I was left behind with Dad. Marguerite was all tears and promises to stay in touch, and her personal security had to peel her off me to haul her away.

"Go," I said, because I was thirteen and stupid, and sure it would be okay. "I'll see you soon."

But that was the last time I saw her in person.

Dad took the divorce badly, and after Mom took Marguerite away, he buried himself in his art. He'd never been as driven as Mom was—she was the Graves, and he just married into the family. So he went back to his work as a sculptor. To being the man he'd been before he fell in love with an heiress, I guess, though he did still live in a mansion, surrounded by staff.

He shut himself away from everything, including me.

He ignored the parts of our empire he was meant to be running, and I was dumped at boarding school, helpless to do anything about it.

I tried *everything* to reach my sister, but it was like Mom had made her disappear off the face of the planet. To Mom's credit, she and Dad had always made sure Marguerite and I were kept out of the public eye. So while my mom was constantly in the news, or giving interviews, I didn't expect to spot my twin on TV.

I called, texted, messaged on multiple systems, used all the old code back doors we'd left for secret messages when we were kids. I tried paying staff to pass actual, physical letters written on literal paper to her. I flew a friend to Mumbai, where I heard she was, to try to deliver a message in person. I even hacked the Graves corporate system to try to reach her.

Nothing. But then Marguerite started showing up in the media. There was coverage about Mom and her going to this country or that, attending meetings together, making moves.

They never mentioned me at all—Mom's other child, my sister's twin. It was like I was invisible, and nobody even remembered I'd been there.

It was about a year after they separated us that a gossip site reported that my sister was staying at Claridge's in London. I'd gotten really good at illegal comms by then, and I got a vid call into her room via the hotel's security system. When Marguerite's face filled the screen—gold-green eyes staring out at me, cheeks pink like she was just in from a run, hair half out of its braid—my heart stopped.

"Marguerite," I whispered, lifting one hand like I could touch her face, instead of the screen.

She blinked at me in pure surprise. "How did you get a call through?" she asked.

And that was when I realized there was a party going on in her hotel suite. Music was thumping low and fast, bodies were moving, someone was shouting, someone else was singing.

Marguerite wasn't being held against her will. She wasn't trapped at this hotel. She was happy. She was *thriving*.

And as we stared at each other, her question hanging in the air between us, it clicked into place. The realization felt like cold water washing over me in a crashing wave—like I couldn't see or hear properly.

I had been so, *so* stupid.

I'd thought we were competing for Mom's attention as a team. But at some point during the months of back-and-forth between Mom and Dad, Marguerite had decided we were up against each other. And worst of all, she'd been right.

She'd planned this, right down to letting me take the hit for her on the hacking job. After that, Mom had let my twin step up to take her place as the Graves heir, always at her side. Marguerite had written her own ticket out, and left me behind.

We'd been playing two different games, my sister and I.

Her lips parted on the vid screen, as though she was about to say something, but I cut the call before she got the chance to lie to my face.

After that, I let my own ambition take over, which is what I should have been doing from the start. I left the boarding school Dad had stashed me at and came home. I hired my own tutors, bringing in staff who could focus on teaching me everything I needed to become a shark like my mother. Like my sister.

I forced my way into meetings, and took over the sections of GravesUP my father had taken in the divorce but effectively abandoned. I used my muscle as a Graves to run them in reality, even if his board members and execs still seemed to be steering the ship on paper.

I made enemies, but I didn't care, though I should have.

I've been in control of those businesses and their billions for four years now, since I was fourteen, which probably sounds wild—but this is what it means to be a Graves. This is the legacy my grandfather left, with his great deeds. To be a Graves, you have to find a way to leave your mark.

I thought I was getting one over on Mom and Marguerite. That one day I'd be able to show my mother what I'd done, how *much* I'd done all on my own. I might have been invisible in the media—they only ever report on the parties I attend, girls I'm seeing—but I was going to be very real in all the ways my mother cares about.

I was waiting for the day I could walk her through the years I'd spent running whole arms of the family empire. I was ready for the moment she'd bring me back in, and let me take on even more parts of this company that changes the world every day.

Marguerite had been learning by her side? Whatever. I'd done it all on my own.

I was ready to bump my sister aside as her heir. But there was one contingency I didn't plan for.

Dad's death.

Now, as I contemplate the low odds of a touching family reunion in the near future, I'm carefully submerging myself in the Pax system, creeping through each section of it like some soldier in one of those movies where they cruise along underwater with only their eyes showing, then jump out and pull off some badass attack. Only I guess my helmet would be covered in daisies.

The invaders' ops team, which seems to consist of at least two of the four people we saw on the bridge, are methodically working their way through all the registers Pax has in its systems. But why? What kind of information could they be after?

The UN Central Registers keep track of who's who and who's where on Mars. Some sections of the planet are still unclaimed, and if you want to get your hands on one of those, the deal is that you have to (a) find a way to get yourself here from Earth, and then (b) physically occupy the land you want to grab, and (c) register your claim with the UN.

You have to tell the UN everything, from who's in your group to what kind of business you're planning to carry on to your survey results, what kind of natural resources you find, the works.

It's expensive—even for us—to get here, so the registers also reveal the various alliances, nations, and corporations that are pooling their cash to make the trip. And fewer of them are doing it these days, since the only unclaimed land is the stuff that doesn't hold much of value.

Every claim out there involves some kind of alliance, except for the GravesUP territory.

We were first, after all.

My grandfather Michael Graves was a visionary who built

a pile of businesses, and changed just about every part of daily life on Earth. He was in housing, medicine, transport, tech—most people's toothpaste probably has a GravesUP logo on it. And then he was the guy who tore up the United Nations Outer Space Treaty (yes, they actually called it that, ten points for originality) and got things on Mars jump-started thirty-one years ago. *Nobody* thought he could do it—that he could launch a rocket, that he and his team could make it to Mars.

And then one day he'd done it, and everyone else was caught with their pants down.

The Graves family have always been rule-breakers. And honestly, there's every chance that humanity would still be stranded on Earth without someone having made a big move. Say what you will about us—and plenty of people do—but the reality is that humanity needed a lifeboat. *We* actually built one, while everybody else debated what color the paint should be. We didn't just dream it—we did it.

The heavy hitters—the USA, China, Russia, India, and some Euro alliances—were all up within five years of my grandfather's team's first landing, because it turns out that panic-buying a space program is actually more effective than you'd think, provided you have the budget. Then came more corporations, more countries, and finally the UN itself, about a decade after the party began. It took them a while to convince their members to cough up the cash.

The early claimants were called the Red Star Rebels, because they all became rule-breakers, once we were. It was kind of like the old gold rushes, everybody grabbing land for themselves, except for one important difference, which was that in the case of Mars, nobody was already living here.

There are protesters who . . . let's say they don't see my grandfather the way I do. Who think everybody deserves a ride.

To them I say: If the Mars For All crew wants a future on the red planet for all of humanity, they need to let the best of humanity do the building first. Then we'll talk about whether their kind can contribute.

I'm jolted from my thoughts when I nearly open a registry while someone else is still in it, which would show them an additional user they couldn't explain.

"You okay?" I jump at Cleo's voice as she reappears. "You just yanked your hands back from that keyboard like it bit you. Looks like you got into the system?"

"Strolled in."

She folds her arms, and her tattoos seem to twine around each other, like she's some disapproving greenhouse creature. "Don't get too cocky, rich boy."

I shrug. "Humans may settle the solar system, but they will never get better at passwords."

"Why do they even have them here? Why not handprints?"

"For a start, your hands have to be pretty clean, and this is the greenhouse," I reply. "Some places they have them in engineering too, because of all the grease. I'm guessing not here, if you haven't seen them."

She gives me a quick shake of her head.

"Only real problem with them is that they encourage hackers," I continue. "And obviously we wouldn't want that."

She gives me a flicker of a smile, and deep on the inside, I allow myself a mental fist pump. It shouldn't feel this satisfying to make her forget our problems for a millisecond.

"Figure anything out?" she asks, resting her hands on the back of my chair and leaning over my shoulder, her cheek close to mine, which isn't distracting *at all*.

"Hard to say. There has to be a reason they're *here*, specifically. However ineffectual the UN is—no offense—people do still care at least a little bit when someone tries to screw with them. They're, like, the fig leaf. The shield everyone uses to pretend we're all being civilized up here. So I'm asking myself what Pax has that nowhere else does, apart from apparently shit security."

"I follow your logic. Got an answer?"

"The UN Central Registers feel like the obvious choice. There's a lot of confidential information. But what they want to do with them, who knows. And hang on, now one of them's looking at the plant inventory. The life-support stuff—hydrogen, oxygen, this whole section of the base. Environmental controls."

She catches her breath, the same fear running through her that's just tensed my muscles. "They're looking for us?"

"I don't think so, they're not checking security cams or monitors. Maybe they just want to know how all the systems work. Or maybe they want to figure out how to break them into tiny pieces."

"I hate this," she mutters.

"You're not alone."

"I was thinking." She straightens up from where she leaned on my chair. "You know how they say, 'You can run, but you can't hide'? Well, we can't hide unless we just want to crouch here until they blow us up in six hours or so. But maybe we can run? There aren't any long-range vehicles left after the evac, but there are the short-range rovers. We could use one as a lifeboat if we had to. They've got life support, at least. Hell, we could hide in one now. The dust storm's officially rolled in, that would give us cover."

"It would unless they spotted us. Then we'd be running away incredibly slowly—what do those things do, twenty-five kilometers an hour?—and with a limited range. We'd be sitting ducks once the short-range battery ran out and they could just come pick us off."

"Killjoy," she mutters. "We don't . . ." Her voice trails off, and I twist in my chair, suddenly sure she's spotted a threat. But she's just staring into space, curling a lock of red hair slowly around her finger.

"Cleo?"

"There *are* long-range vehicles at the base," she murmurs. "*They* arrived in them."

I blink at her. She's right. "You think we should boost one of their rovers?"

She shrugs. "They'll go far enough to get us to a neighboring base. I think we should at least take a look at them."

"If we're about to steal a car, I think we should break into that pack of cookies we found first, just in case. Blood sugar aids concentration, you know."

"You've never been in actual danger before," she informs me. "And it shows. You eat your cookie, I'll be back in a minute."

She disappears through the doorway that leads to the environmental-control equipment. I briefly consider following her, but . . . I do have those cookies. So I dig them out and crunch my way through one as I wait for Cleo to return.

She reappears with a small remote in one hand and a tiny drone hovering in the air in front of her, almost completely silent. She has a headband on now with an eyepiece flipped out from it, just a transparent screen that sits in front of her left eye.

"Drone has a camera?" I guess.

"Let's let someone else check around the corners for danger," she replies. "Grab a couple of helmets and pass me a cookie."

So I grab the helmets for our suits—can't be too careful about the potential for catastrophic breaches while there are folks running around with guns—and pass her a cookie. Then I follow her into the hallway.

We move quietly, and knowing the drone's checking the way ahead means we can move a lot quicker too. Cleo keeps it up near the ceiling, where it won't be in anyone's line of sight if it buzzes around the corner and into danger. Whatever faint noise it makes is masked by the sound of the fans working in the background.

As we pass the banks of doors, a thought occurs to me. "Where are your quarters? Is there anything you want to take with you? There's no promise this place will still be standing when you come back to it."

Cleo pauses before she replies and it's like she's choosing

her words. "It'd be out of the way," she says after a moment. "There's no need."

And I'll be honest, it's a little weird, the way she says it. Unless you're in the fancy seats, you don't get much of a luggage allotment, coming to Mars. An engineering student sure wouldn't. Whatever she brought would have meant a lot to her. I brought my favorite piece of my dad's work. It's a small, delicate sculpture in soapstone, all wistful curves, and it took up a full third of my own luggage allotment.

Why doesn't she want to go get whatever piece of her heart she brought with her?

Does she think we're going to die?

We head about a quarter of the way around the circular tunnel that marks the edge of the base, and we don't speak again until we reach the balcony overlooking the maintenance garage. From up here, we should be able to see the east garage door without being seen.

Cleo calls down the tiny drone, clipping it to her suit. *Too quiet in there*, she mouths, and I nod. Then she eases the door open with agonizing slowness, her ear pressed to the gap. Once she's satisfied there's nobody on the other side, she slides it open just enough to pass through, and carefully sinks down to lie on her stomach. She wriggles forward with all the speed of a heavily sedated snail. She doesn't make a sound. Feels like she's being overly cautious, given the absolute silence on the other side of the door, but I don't argue.

Instead I set down the helmets I'm carrying just inside the

door and copy her, the cold metal pressing against my borrowed T-shirt and chilling my skin, my legs protected by the thick fabric of the pressure suit. We ooze across to the edge of the balcony like a couple of perfectly silent assassin slugs and then, incredibly carefully, take a strategic peek over the edge.

The room below is a large quarter circle, with individual garages along the curved edge of the room, and repair equipment packed onto the two straight walls that angle in to meet at the entrance—that part's out of sight beneath our balcony.

Each of the vehicles is housed in the same kind of garage I saw when I so nearly got a ride out of here. *Curse you, Patrick, for showing up to claim your seat.* It's an airlock arrangement, where they can drive in from the outside, a door seals behind them, and then once the chamber has pressurized, the inner door opens to let the passengers walk through into the base itself.

Cleo taps me on the arm and points to a mercenary sitting still and silent against one wall. He's chewing on what looks like a protein bar as he gazes into space, like he's idly waiting for something.

I hadn't even seen him, and a jolt of adrenaline goes through me, bringing with it a flash of nausea as I realize how easily I could have said something and given us away. As I gaze down at him, my breath catches in my throat, as though he might hear even a quiet exhalation. He looks like he's daydreaming, but I have no doubt he's alert for exactly the kind of noise I'd have made if Cleo hadn't slowed me down.

I look across at her, and she holds up both hands, extending her fingers until she's counted to seven. It takes me a second to understand what she means. Then my gut drops.

This guy isn't one of the four mercs we saw on the bridge—his skin is a deeper brown than any of theirs, and even though he's sitting down, I can tell he's Martian tall, born here and raised in low gravity. The rest of them looked Earthborn to me. He's not one of the pair we glimpsed in the corridor either.

That means there are at least seven of them. And two of us. I do not like these odds. I would *very* much like to steal one of these rovers and run like hell.

Footsteps sound below and a woman comes striding in. Beside me, Cleo flinches, her shoulder pressing against mine. If she's thinking this is eight, though, she's wrong—we saw this woman catch a gun back on the bridge. She's got a tattoo that runs across her forehead like a tiara, and I doubt there are two the same in the crew.

"Sabrina," the man below says, rising to his feet. Sure enough, he's more than a head taller than her. "About damn time."

"Shut up," she replies lazily, following him over to a large crate and then looking him up and down with a grin. "Damn, are you always snacking?"

"Takes a lot to fuel this," he replies, stuffing his bar in his suit pocket and gesturing to his lanky self. "What kept you?"

"I was taking a look at the setup in person. This would be a lot easier at home, you know. They're kind of obsessive about fire in space."

"You try living somewhere without any atmosphere," the

Martian replies as they hoist the crate together, him stooping to try to match her height. "Makes you kind of twitchy. So can you do it?"

"Oh sure. The environmental-control system has a bunch of redundancies, but it all comes back to just two locations that matter. I can override them, pump the oxygen levels sky-high."

"That won't, you know, brain damage us?" he asks, trying to sound casual and not really succeeding.

"We'd need to stick around a lot longer than we plan to, for that to happen. I've already rigged the oxygenators to start overproducing. All it'll take is a spark after that. I'll be ready in time."

"Six and a half hours to go," he tells her, with a grin I hate already.

Neither Cleo nor I say a word as Sabrina and the Martian carry the crate out of sight, and we wait a full minute longer, just to be sure they're gone. To be honest, I think both of us need the minute to recover from what we just heard.

"Environmental controls," Cleo mutters then, dropping her head to rest it on her hands.

My insides have gone cold, and I swear I can feel my heart beating in my chest, my blood pushing through my veins.

"This is incredibly bad," I say slowly. "If they adjust the enviro controls to flood this place with oxygen, she's right that it'll only take a spark. Fire will rip through here like a bomb's gone off. Wherever there's air, it'll be lethal."

"And it'll destroy the systems she hacked, so there won't be a trace they were ever here," Cleo murmurs. "All the more reason to get into one of those rovers right now." She hauls herself to her feet, climbs over the railing in a quick movement, then lowers herself down to drop to the floor below, landing with impossible lightness.

Only it's not impossible, because we're in about a third of Earth's gravity. Of course.

I rise to my feet, ducking back to grab our helmets. One at a time I drop them down to her. Then I swing one leg over the railing and switch my grip before bringing my other leg over too. I lower myself until I'm hanging, and it's the strangest feeling—I have Earth-level muscles, but I only weigh a third as much. I try for a quick chin-up, and . . . yeah. Mars gravity is good for the ego.

"If you're done admiring yourself, get down here," Cleo hisses, and I drop to the ground in surprise. Despite the quick flash of adrenaline that warns me I'm falling too far, I land lightly on my feet. This is going to take some getting used to.

Together we hurry across the bay to where the nearest rover is docked. I peer through the airlock window, and Cleo crowds in alongside me. The rover waiting for us is battered, but fine. And like the suits our invaders wear, it has no markings.

"I guess we have to short the door to get through," I say quietly. "Once we do that, they'll know someone's here. Let's talk through the exact steps we'll take—quickly—so we can move as fast as possible once we start. If we can just get a few minutes' head start and drive well, we should be able to keep ahead until we can radio the nearest settlements."

"Not so fast, rich boy," Cleo mutters. "I think we have another problem to solve first. Boost me up on your shoulders."

"You want to what?" I blink at her, but her scowl gets me moving—she has a hot, bossy thing going on that I did *not* know I found this interesting—and I drop to one knee, bowing my head so she can climb aboard. In this gravity, she weighs almost nothing.

I push up to stand, and absolutely don't notice Cleo's thighs locking around my neck. I make myself recite a list of GravesUP Industries patents. Alphabetically.

"Can I ask what you're doing, or would that just be getting in the way?" I venture, as she leans in to rest her hands against the window, examining the rover from above.

"I'm getting a look at the dashboard," she replies. "No point breaking in and then realizing we can't start it."

"Fair."

She lets out a slow breath. "Hunter." Her voice is heavy.

My gut drops. "No, don't say it."

She rests her forehead against the window above me. "We can't start it. It's handprint activated."

"Okay, well, I don't feel great about cutting off someone's hand," I say, reaching for a way to lighten the mood as I begin to back away so she can climb down. *Leadership, Hunter. We can't afford despair.*

"Cutting off a hand wouldn't work. The system can sense if there's no circulation." She hits the ground and turns her head to catch my horrified expression.

"And you know that why?"

"It was a joke," she replies, with a roll of her eyes. "Also, you know. Engineers know this stuff."

"I've been hanging out with some very boring engineers," I tell her. "What now?"

"Now we stop standing out in the open and discussing our problems. Let's take it somewhere a little more private."

10.

CLEO

6 HOURS, 30 MINUTES REMAINING

"I HATE THIS," HUNTER mutters.

"You're not alone."

We've let ourselves into the Yang family's living quarters—according to a hand-decorated nameplate by the door—and are talking in whispers.

The room is small, similar to the first living quarters we snuck into. Two sets of bunk beds line the walls, coming together at a right angle. A huge shelf stuffed with personal possessions lines the third. The fourth contains the door, plus a messy gallery of hand-painted art.

I'm lying on a bunk, and Hunter is prowling around like some huge caged animal.

Whatever we do, I have to keep him close. I'll have a better chance of coming through this with a partner—even one who's had little to no contact with the real world. And one way or another, he'll be useful at the end of this, either as my ticket to the GravesUP compound or as an incredibly valuable asset to trade for my own freedom.

And if that sounds harsh, remember that he's got a family who'll pay any amount of money to get him back. He'd never be a hostage for long.

If there's one thing I've learned so far in life, it's this: Nobody's coming to get me, so I have to save myself.

And in the meantime, he's not hard to look at.

"So," says Hunter, swinging around to face me. "Let's work the problem. We've established we can't hide, because even if that works, all we'll do is buy ourselves just under six and a half hours. Then they'll light a spark, and we'll go up with this place."

"Right," I agree. "And we can't run. We can't steal a ride out of here, unless we can find a way to get one of them to cooperate long enough to start a rover for us. Tricky, when they're the ones with the guns."

Sabrina. Her name flashes into my mind as I think back to the maintenance bay. I wonder if she'd believe me if I told her who Hunter was.

"Cleo?" Hunter's looking at me, and I realize I've missed something he said.

"Sorry, thought I had an idea, but it's nothing. What were you saying?"

"I asked if you see any other options, besides trying to . . . whatever we want to call it. Stop them."

I let out a slow breath. "Not right now, but you'll be the first to know if inspiration hits. What does 'stop them' mean?"

He bites the inside of his cheek, his gaze flickering over the domesticity of the living quarters, as though he might find something to help him answer the question. "It means kill them, I guess. It's what they'll do to us if they can."

"How would we even begin to kill seven people?" I ask, lifting my hands to scrub at my face.

"How would we kill *one*?" he whispers. "I don't know if I can. I've never even hurt anyone. I mean, I do self-defense classes, but . . ."

You might not have hurt people, I want to say, *but your family has killed people, even if it wasn't with their bare hands. Every cent you'll inherit is built on killing people. And you don't even know it.*

My father's face flashes before my eyes for a moment, tight with pain. I see his hands—always callused, usually smudged with grease and oil—shaking, when once they were so steady. He was a mechanic, and fascinated by every kind of machine. He's the reason I can hot-wire a workstation in under ten seconds. And GravesUP is the reason he's gone.

"Cleo?" Hunter says again. And then, so kindly you'd never know he was the son of a monster: "You don't look great, all of a sudden. Are you feeling okay? It's been one terrifying shock after another, right? How's your blood sugar? We've got the cookies, or there are some instant noodles over here, and a pressure kettle. I think we can risk a tiny power draw to make some up."

"I've never killed anyone either," I say, instead of *I've never hurt anyone*. "I'll take a cookie."

And please don't be kind. Bargaining chips aren't kind.

He crosses over to where I lie on the bunk, and I shift my legs so he can sink down slowly to sit beside me. He digs through his bag for the cookies.

I study him while he's distracted, and something softens in me as I do. He has broad shoulders, the T-shirt's fabric stretched across them. There's a curl at the nape of his neck that I want to tuck back into place amid the rest of his tousled hair. *What?* A girl can look.

"So we're not killers," he says. "Maybe we try for something else, first. We look for a way to put them at some kind of disadvantage that means they're willing to bargain with us. Or just means they can't do whatever they came here to do. Have you read *The Art of War*?"

"Let's assume I haven't," I reply, heroically resisting a roll of my eyes.

"It's an ancient book about strategy. It says that when you're badly outnumbered, you should avoid direct confrontation. Force the enemy into engagements where they can only take you on a few at a time. Confuse them. Separate them from each other."

"If we can do that, maybe we actually can force a rover out of one of them," I murmur. "If they don't know what's going on, or where the danger's coming from."

"Exactly. They don't know this place," he points out. "You've been here awhile, and you *do* know your way around, which is an advantage. Plus, you're great with hardware. You can wire up power sources as we need them, get machinery started. I don't know this place any better than they do, but I *do* know the software. I know how it runs. I'm better with the systems than anyone on their team, no question."

"Okay, that's not nothing to work with," I admit.

"They don't know we're here, that's another advantage. They're not expecting resistance. I think we make it look like accidents, for as long as we can," he says slowly. "So they take a little longer to be on their guard."

Huh. Hunter Graves is a lot of things, but I'm coming to the realization that he's not stupid. He's thinking tactically. Maybe all those hostile takeovers were good practice.

There's a strange sort of . . . is this hope, waking up inside me?

If it is, then it's drowned out a moment later when the urge to laugh overwhelms it.

"What's . . . ?" He looks down at me, bewildered, then pulls the cookies out of his bag, opening the packet to offer one to me.

"I'm sorry," I manage, taking the cookie and turning it over in my hand. "I just realized we're sitting here in some random family's bedroom, talking about our two-person rebellion against a crack mercenary team, while we eat cookies. We're not action heroes. We're insane."

"Well," he says, with an answering grin, "sounds like we've got the element of surprise on our side, anyway. Who would expect someone to do something as stupid as that?" He reaches for my free hand tentatively, slow enough that I could pull away, or just move, and the moment would pass.

I let him take it. After all, we need to bond.

His skin is warm as his fingers curl gently around mine.

"Here we go," he says softly. "We'll do it together."

I let myself squeeze his hand. "Let's get started."

11.

CLEO

5 HOURS, 54 MINUTES REMAINING

A PRECIOUS THIRTY MINUTES later, I'm wading through the water that's slowly filling classroom 3, watching it slosh around the feet of my pressure suit.

The students were mid-class when the evacuation signal came in, and before we could get to work we had to clear away an in-progress science experiment that should *not* have been left unattended. These kids need better hazard training.

Now the room is gradually filling with water; the taps are running as fast as they can, and the sinks are all plugged. They overflowed as planned, and the water's rippling across the floor every time I move. We weren't sure if the door seals would stand up to this, but almost every room on the base is designed to become an airlock if required, and so far the good ship *Science Class* has remained watertight.

"Where did you *get* this idea?" Hunter asks as he climbs up onto a desk.

"An ex of mine," I say, checking the taps can't run any faster. "She came up with it to humble a bunch of jocks at school, and my dad taught us how to execute it."

"Electrical engineer?" Hunter guesses.

Mechanic and fix-it guy. "Something like that. He probably should have asked more questions about what we were planning to do with the information."

Hunter snickers. "What happened to the jocks?"

"Flooded their locker room, left them stranded in the showers. Naked."

He laughs properly, a warm, easy sound. Then carefully—soooooo carefully—he hoists himself into the ventilation pipe above us.

He's not moving slowly because it's difficult. The much lighter Martian gravity means that his problem is too much strength, not too little. Pull himself up too fast, and he'll smash his head into the ceiling. I thought I was keeping up my exercise while I was here, but watching him now, I'm not so sure.

The way he moves does something to my insides that I'd rather wasn't happening, and the way his shirt rides up to give me a look at his abs is frankly just gratuitous and unnecessary. He probably practices that in the mirror.

He disappears headfirst into the ventilation pipe with a quick kick of his feet. The ventilation system is like a big tube clamped onto the ceiling, and he only just fits.

Once I'm sure he's not going to ruin my beautiful smile with another kick, I climb onto the table and reach up to grab the edge of the square hole in the vent with both hands.

I'm smaller than Hunter, but it's still not much wider than my shoulders in there. As I heave myself up and in, and the light immediately dims, I shiver.

I shuffle back and forth across the opening until I'm settled with my head toward the hole I came up through, and my feet toward Hunter. A soft *oof* tells me my feet have connected with some part of my partner in crime, so I stop there, and reach down through the opening to pull the duct cover up.

Wondering what I'm doing? I bet you are. Keep watching.

"Pass me the wires?" I say softly.

"Coming through. Careful."

I reach my hand back as far as I can, and Hunter strains forward to press the coil of insulated wires against my palm. I ease them forward *very* carefully, past my body, until I can set the loop of wires on top of the duct cover, making sure the live end doesn't touch the grate. The pipe we're in *shouldn't* conduct electricity, but I'd rather not test that theory.

"Screwdriver?"

"Screwdriver," he says, like some kind of surgeon's assistant, passing it forward. Our hands brush as I reach back for it, and he presses his fingertips against mine. On purpose? Maybe.

Slowly, carefully, I start to unfasten the screws that keep the duct's hinges in place. My chest feels tight, and I try a deeper, slow breath, but it's as if my lungs refuse to expand. I never used to have a problem with small spaces, until I launched from Earth crammed into a packing box.

The crew member who smuggled me on sprayed foam all around me to help counter the gravity of takeoff, and its spongy texture locked my limbs into place, my face turned up to breathe as he hammered the lid down hard.

I still dream, sometimes, about the roar and the vibrations of that moment. About the fear that he might just not come back, and I'd be stuck there, trapped like a fly in a web. I do *not* like to rely on others.

"All right?" Hunter asks, catching me by surprise.

"Tight fit," I mutter. "It's fine."

"Well, let me know if you want a foot massage while you work," he jokes, and though I give a little kick to warn him, I'm also glad the dark hides the smile he draws out of me.

He pays more attention than I expect him to, this boy. The world parts around him when he moves, and I'd expect him to just stride ahead without even noticing. But he sees things, Hunter Graves.

"So," I say, reaching for distraction, and remembering I'm supposed to be bonding with Hunter—I can multitask—"your mom's at the GravesUP compound? Has it been a long time since you saw her?"

"About five years," Hunter replies, quiet in the dim light. "Earth years, not Martian. Only about"—he pauses to calculate—"two point seven years, Martian. That sounds better."

"She's been on Mars for *five years*?" There's no way that woman has enough strength left in her body to ever return to

Earth, not after five Earth years in light Martian gravity. I'm surprised a CEO at her level would close off that avenue.

"No, she's only been here for one," he says. "She's just had a lot going on."

There's a pause as I search for the right response to his mom's calendar having been too full to see her son for five freaking years. I mean, I know about shitty moms, but his sounds like a real prize. Luckily for me, Hunter fills the silence.

"I was with my dad most of that time."

"I guess you're going to miss him, coming here," I offer as the first screw comes out of the vent cover.

Now it's Hunter's turn to pause. I wait it out. "No," he says eventually. "We kept it out of the news, but he died. Mom doesn't like public displays of vulnerability, so she didn't really want people to know."

"Oh, shit. Sorry." And I am. Graves or not, I know exactly what it's like to lose your dad. And to have a mom who cuts you loose.

I can't help wondering how a member of the Graves family could possibly get so sick that they couldn't pay their way out of it, though.

"He was killed," Hunter says, as if reading my mind. Or perhaps people always wonder. *Always? How many people has he told?* "It was protesters," he continues. "Mars For All."

"What did—" I catch myself mid-sentence. "Why did they target him?" Not *what did he do?*, though he probably did.

"No reason, apart from marrying into the Graves family," Hunter whispers. "They wanted my mother's attention. My father was an artist." His voice cracks on that husky whisper with something fierce—a sharp grief, an anger that's still burning bright.

"I'm so sorry," I say again, which is such a useless response. But there's a reason everyone always says it—there's nothing better you can replace it with. Because nothing really helps.

"I saw it," Hunter says softly. "He was coming back from some charity thing, and I was out on the front steps of our house to meet him. His motorcade blew up just as it came through our gates. There was this fireball, and his car flew into the air. It kept turning over and over . . . By the time I got to the car, I could hear him screaming inside, and then he stopped."

And his mother stayed on Mars, leaving her son to get through that alone. I don't let myself say that out loud. If Hunter doesn't want to see that choice for what it is, now isn't the time to rub his nose in it.

I wish I could take his hand, but all I can do is stretch my arm back, silent. I can't even turn my head.

After a moment, his fingers brush against mine. "It was about six months ago," he says, his whisper still rough. "I'm not good at telling the story yet."

I do *not* want to feel sorry for the sad billionaire in the ventilation tunnel behind me, but honestly, this is a lot.

"I can't imagine how they ever thought killing him would get your mother to cooperate," I murmur. "If I were her, I'd want to retaliate."

"I think she does," he agrees. "Mars For All says Mars should be open to more people. They think corporations and countries should have to sponsor more people who can't self-fund. And they want forgiveness for any hitchers who make it here. But it turns out one of the people responsible for the blast was a hitcher who'd been deported from Mars. It came out in the hearings." He draws in a slow, shuddering breath, and steadies himself. "The irony is, until then, I'd actually been wondering if they had a point, the Mars For All crew. If maybe we should look for ways to broaden the criteria for getting a seat on a ship. That maybe there was talent we were missing. Ways that everyday people help create the culture of a place—I mean, I've met executives. Then Mars For All showed me what kind of people they really are. Who they speak for. I hope we hunt down every last one of them and send them home."

The air goes out of my lungs as a cocktail of sympathy and despair swirls inside me, and I close my eyes.

Those people who don't deserve to be here, the ones who didn't earn or pay for a place, the hitchers who should all be deported? I'm one of them. And clearly all hitchers are the same to him.

People like me killed his father, who he loved. And I want to say, *Do you think there's a reason they were so desperate?* Or maybe, *Are you going to punish the ones who were never violent, just because a few were?* He's never going to help me, once he figures out who I am. He watched his father die just months ago.

I try to steady myself. I have to say something, to break the tension singing in the air after his last words. "Your mom must be looking forward to having you here," I try. "To being together after everything."

Hunter's quiet for a long moment, and I wish I could see his face. Eventually he speaks. "You know how I said they don't know I made it to Pax?" He lets out a slow breath. "They also don't know I made it to Orbital. They don't know I'm here at all. I bribed my way onto a freighter."

I bang my head on the roof of the tube when I try to do a double take. "Wait, they think you're on *Earth*? She didn't notice that you'd gone silent for *four months*? What about your sister?"

"We don't talk," he replies, in what's trying so hard to be a neutral tone, but comes out grim. "Lucky, really. She'd have told my mother immediately, and getting yelled at with transmissions on a twenty-minute time delay, both ways, would have been an ordeal."

"Still, Hunter, you can't seriously—"

"Oh, I hear how it sounds," he agrees. "But this was my only option. I've spent the last few years quietly running my father's arms of the business—they didn't interest him. I was going to use all that work to prove to my mother that I deserve a place in the Graves family business. But I pissed off a lot of people, forcing my way onto those boards, into those meetings. So the minute Dad was gone, his executive officers shoved me aside and erased the fact that I'd ever been there."

"So showing up unannounced is about, what, taking some of that power back?"

"Being a Graves is about legacy. We've changed the world for the better, and I'm going to be a part of all the changes to come. But now everything I did to show I'm ready to step up is gone. What's left is to force a confrontation with my mother. To talk her through everything I've been doing and *make* her see what I'm capable of. To convince her to let me in. My sister's been at her side all this time, setting herself up as the only rightful heir. I have to roll the dice, if I want what's mine."

Marguerite Graves. I've heard her name. I've seen her quotes in the news, if not her picture. She's always seemed like she'd punch you in the face, then charge you for her time.

I wonder if she looks like her brother.

I need to change the subject from the Graves legacy before I ask him whose world, exactly, they've changed for the better. The one thing I can't do is argue with him outright.

"Soooo," I say slowly, squinching one eye open, as if I can see his face while I take this risk. "You lied your way up here, huh. Makes you a kind of hitcher, doesn't it?"

Hunter laughs abruptly, a surprised sound, and his hand finds my ankle to give it a squeeze. "Damn, you make a good point. I swear, as soon as I can find someone in authority, I'll hand myself in. So what's your story? You said before that you were here alone. Are your family coming later?"

I should have seen that question coming. But I'm still caught up in the tangle of his father's death, and Hunter's ambitions, and the fact that his mother is as terrible as mine—and he surprises me into answering with the truth.

"I don't have any family. I lost my dad too, actually." My fingers are still gripping the grate, holding it in place where I took the screws out, and my whole hand's starting to clench and ache.

Now it's Hunter's turn. "Oh, shit, Cleo, I'm so sorry. You shouldn't have let me go on about—"

"Don't be," I mutter. "It was years ago. There were a lot of medical bills left behind afterwards. We lost everything, and we still owed money. And after that . . . well, maybe you'll get it, actually. Your mother doesn't sound like a treat, if you don't mind me saying so. No contact for five years is a lot."

"That's fair. I'm guessing yours isn't up for Mom of the Year either?"

"She'd probably pawn the trophy." I snort. "Mine lumped me with all the medical debt, since I was a minor. She figured they'd cancel it, instead of going after a teenager. Which was incorrect, by the way. And then she split. I haven't seen her since. I heard she went to Georgia, but who knows."

Hunter's voice is incredulous. "I'm sorry, *what*?"

"Which bit are you having trouble believing? That they'd chase me for the debt before I hit eighteen, that my mother split, or that she went to Georgia? They really cleaned it up after the whole thing with the reactor. I heard it's pretty safe these days."

"Uh, take your pick, I guess," he manages.

"Look, not to sound . . ." *Like I think you're a sheltered rich boy.* "That's how life goes, where I come from," I say quietly. "Nobody I grew up with would be surprised by that story. It taught me a lot about not relying on other people. I figured the debt collectors wouldn't track me off-world, so I got my apprenticeship—"

"Engineering, right," he agrees, probably wondering how I afforded any of the education I'd need for that, if I grew up somewhere that taught me the kinds of lessons I've learned. Which is a fair question, because I couldn't afford it.

"Yeah, engineering. And I came here. Only to find myself hiding out in a ventilation shaft with my new friend Hunter Graves, missing the good old days of debt collectors threatening to smash in my knees. What a weird day."

My mind obligingly flashes on the breathless desperation of running down an alleyway, the debt collectors' footsteps—Sabrina's footsteps—pounding behind me.

Every moment of that was because of this boy and his family, I remind myself.

Hunter sighs, and I think the thunk I hear is his head hitting the floor of the pipe we're stuffed inside. "What was it like here?" he asks, slightly muffled. "Before the whole life-threatening-danger situation?"

I watch the water through the grille of the duct cover I'm holding in place. It's still flowing steadily, spilling down the sides of the cabinets in small waterfalls and rippling out until it hits the far wall. (I know, you're curious. Not long now, with any luck.)

I'm trying to think about what kind of answer works best for the person I'm supposed to be right now—what would make sense for an apprentice engineer to say. What might make him sympathetic, although—and the knowledge hits me in the gut again—he won't be helping me anytime soon, once he figures out I'm a hitcher.

But weirdly, mostly what I want to do is tell him the truth, even though that's a bad idea.

"It hasn't been what I hoped," I say eventually, when I realize I've taken too long to reply. "I'm not sure it was a good idea to come, even if I was in danger back home. I thought I was on my own there—I sure felt like I was—but at least I knew people. Here, I've been really alone, these last few months. And I don't know what to do next."

His hand tightens on my ankle again, and I wish I could feel the warmth of it through my suit. "Cleo, if we get out of this—"

"*When* we get out of this," I correct him.

"Of course, when we get out of this," he repeats obediently.

"Glad to hear you're accepting some leadership, rich boy." I can hear myself joking, hear myself teasing him, but there's this huge gulf between us, and he doesn't even know it's there.

"*When* we get out of this," he forges on. "You can write your own ticket to the GravesUP compound, or anywhere we're connected to. I'll help you find any position you want. And if you want to go back to Earth, I'll have the debts taken care of and find you a ride."

A strange, detached shock flows through me, like a weird kind of grief. This is exactly what I wanted. If you'd told me yesterday that I'd get this offer, I'd have done backflips. But now I know he won't give it to me, not really.

Maybe if I can get to Graves before he finds out who I really am, I'll have a chance of hiding there—but something tells me they'll be a lot more efficient than the UN at sniffing out hitchers.

I'm searching for words when the alarm kicks in below. A red light starts to flash near the door, and a low, mournful *whoop* echoes around the classroom. The ventilation shaft vibrates with the noise, but I have to keep hold of the grille, so I can't block my ears. The noise ricochets around my head, and I can feel it in my temples, my jaw.

Hopefully an alarm's going off on the bridge as well, and in a minute we'll have the company we've been waiting for. Honestly, the water should have set off an alarm ages ago; it must be over ankle-deep down there. *Pax, you desperately need more funding.*

Hunter and I both go quiet, and I shift my grip on the grate cover again. I can't drop it too soon—this is going to be all about timing. Thankfully, it only takes a minute before the door opens, and I get my first close-up look at another of the mercenaries.

This isn't the Martian, or Sabrina. This is the woman we first saw on the bridge, unpacking the guns. She has black hair with blue streaks dyed all through it, pulled back in a braid that hangs halfway down her back. She's probably a spacer—her skin is that kind of almost translucent white that says it's never seen the sun, and when her eyes dart around the room, I catch blue sparks in them that are probably vision augments of some kind.

As soon as Blue Braid opens the door, water starts to flood out through it. Cursing, she hustles inside and pulls the door shut after her, rather than let the water flow out into the hallway. So far, so good—we were hoping she'd be smart enough to do that.

To all our relief, she flips up the cover on the alarm button by the door and smacks it to silence the whooping siren. Then she sloshes over to the sinks and shuts off the water, before turning to take in the classroom. "What in the seven hells were these kids doing?" she mutters to herself.

I loosen my grip on the grate—my hand's so tense from curling into a claw that for a moment I think I won't be able to straighten my fingers. But the cover drops into the water, and Blue Braid whips around at the splash.

Then I grab for the coil of wire, and begin to unspool it, letting the first wires slither down toward the water.

We both agreed we had to at least give her a chance to see what was about to happen. Hopefully it'll look like the construction crew left the wires coiled on top of the duct, because build crews everywhere are slackers, and everything's harder in a suit, so you're looking for shortcuts. And now the humidity or something—she won't have time to think—has caused the vent cover to pop out, and bad things are about to happen.

Good news: She's not stupid. She takes one look at the wires spooling down toward the floor, spits a curse, and jumps up onto a desk, no doubt hoping that whatever it's made of doesn't conduct electricity.

The second she's up there I drop the wires, and they spark as they make contact with the water. Then everything goes quiet. Blue Braid knows what's up, though. She knows the water around the base of her desk is electrified now, conducting whatever current was in the wires that fell. She stays right where she is, easing down to sit on the desk like she's planning a long stay.

I start scooting back along the pipe, resisting the urge to cackle with glee. Good luck to them, figuring how to get her out.

If Blue Braid's friends open the door, electrified water will come pouring out. They'll have to figure out how to shut off the power to the whole section, and that should take them a minute.

Meanwhile, Hunter and I will see how many others we can isolate before they get her free. If we can rattle them, whittle them down, maybe we really can force one into starting a rover for us.

Hunter must be moving backward behind me, but for a big guy, he's silent. I press my hands to the floor of the pipe and gently slide myself backward again, toward the junction where we can escape.

Below, Blue Braid's voice rings out, and I freeze.

"Leader, this is six. I'm in the classroom, checking on that humidifier alarm. Listen, the whole room's flooded, and the water's electrified."

There's a moment's silence, and I can only imagine the questions the Pirate is firing at her down the line. *What did you say?* Probably followed closely by *How are you alive? Am I speaking to a ghost right now?*

"I'm standing on a desk. It's nonconductive. Look, that's not what's important."

Another pause. I'm guessing: *You don't think being trapped by a tiny electrified lake is important? How are we supposed to get you out of there?*

"Listen, I'd appreciate it if someone figured that out, but we have bigger issues. The wires that hit the water came down out of the ventilation shaft. And I only had a moment to look, but I'm absolutely sure I saw movement up there."

Fear sweeps through me in a wave. I'm frozen in place, and behind me I hear the softest intake of breath from Hunter. Neither of us moves. *Shit, those blue sparks in her eyes* were *vision augments.*

"I *can't* shoot," Blue Braid says. "I don't know what that vent's made of. I don't want anything ricocheting back on me. Not while I'm stuck on this damn desk. But you might want to figure out where this vent ends up, because whatever the evac logs said, I don't think we're alone here."

My body's locked in place, my muscles aching from clenching so hard. This isn't fight or flight—this is the other option they forget to tell you about, *freeze*. It's like I'm trapped inside myself, screaming that I need to move, I need to run, but I don't know how. I can't even make my little finger move.

Then Hunter's hand closes gently around my ankle one more time, and it's like I *can* feel the warmth of his skin through my suit—like it races up my leg, and somehow thaws me.

I begin to move again, shuffling back slowly and quietly—I don't want to give her a sound that will confirm what she already believes.

But in my mind, I'm ten steps ahead, my old instincts pushing up from below the surface.

It's time to do what I always end up doing.

It's time to run.

12.

HUNTER

5 HOURS, 38 MINUTES REMAINING

I SCRAMBLE FRANTICALLY TOWARD the junction, shoving myself backward through the ventilation pipe. Then I drop down through the duct, feet-first, praying there's nobody waiting for me.

The storage room is empty, and I stumble back when I hit the floor, colliding with a packing crate as Cleo jumps down after me, arms windmilling for balance.

The second she's on her feet I spin toward the door that leads to the greenhouse, but Cleo grabs for my arm, yanking me back.

"More hallways this way," she raps out, tilting her head toward the opposite door. "More places to lose them."

"But we know the route this way," I argue, pointing back at the door we came through.

She studies me for a long second, then lets go of her grip on my arm and simply turns to smack the release beside her door panel and disappear through it at a run.

Cursing under my breath, I do exactly what she's betting on, and run after her.

She leads me through a series of storage rooms, all linked together, all piled high with boxes and leftover materials. On Mars, they never throw *anything* out—after all, you have to either ship it in or manufacture it here, if you end up wishing later that you hadn't gotten rid of it.

Neither of us speaks—the only soundtrack is the soft, steady thud of our footsteps, and the rasp of our breath. My senses are hyperalert, straining for the smallest sign that someone's on our tail, or up ahead, or about to burst through a door.

Ahead of me, Cleo ducks past a sheet of plastic that's hanging to separate a half-renovated room and grabs a support column to swing herself around toward a door.

Did she get this good running from debt collectors? No wonder she calls me *rich boy*. It's all anyone sees when they look at me, I do know that. But for Cleo, it must be so unimaginably different from her life. It must seem like I can fly.

Since Dad died and my life imploded, I've been furious that I've got everything anyone could want, except the one thing *I* want. Surrounded by riches but shut out by my family.

Watching the way Cleo instantly takes flight, seeing the way it's an instinct for her, I'm realizing there are worse things than being rich but alone. I could just be alone.

We break out into a hallway, and it must be the huge ring corridor that circles the base—it has the same long, slow curve, the same lights set into the ceiling. I stumble after her, throwing a hand out to drag along the wall, trying to stop myself from falling. Running in low gravity is like constantly falling forward—fast, as long as you don't need to change direction or stop.

We approach a major intersection, where someone's tried to make it homey. There are crates piled up to sit on like park benches, a fake tree, and a pole with street signs pointing in every possible direction, listing distances to other settlements and compounds: EURO W, EURO E, GRAVESUP, FREYACO, AFRO U, ARES TECH, and even EARTH.

As we dash across the intersection, a voice rings out from one of the other corridors. "There! Target ahead!"

An instant later a blast rings out, and the plastic crate nearest me shatters, shrapnel flying as a bullet hits it. I dive over the crates, landing in an awkward roll that sends a bolt of pain up my spine, and somehow scramble to my feet.

I grab Cleo's hand as she stumbles, and sling her toward the safety of a corridor—she keeps hold of me and uses her grip to drag me on with her.

There's another blast behind us as we take the next turn—I keep hold of her hand now, and let her steer. We're sprinting toward a huge set of double doors, but suddenly they start to slide slowly closed, with a soft hum and a warning beep.

Someone on the bridge is trying to herd us, corral us somewhere we can't escape.

"They're using the cameras," I gasp. "We have to get out of sight."

Cleo skids to a halt, then ducks sidelong into another room. I'm an instant behind her, and together we burst into a workshop. Like everywhere else on the base, it was abandoned midshift. There's a 3-D printer still running, slowly extruding what was probably meant to be the wall of a hab section. In the time since the evac, it's turned into a rippling sheet of messy build materials, pushing up against a neighboring table and starting to collapse in on itself.

Music's still playing softly from one corner and it masks our footsteps as we hurry past workbenches laden with tools, half of them branded with the shooting stars of the GravesUP logo.

My gaze lands on something shaped like a gun, and I grab for it, then realize it's useless—the only thing it's loaded with is putty or something.

"Yes!" Cleo hisses, her eyes lighting up. "Give."

I don't waste my breath explaining it won't work—we don't have time for that. I just toss it to her. She catches it without breaking stride and jams it into her belt. If she's going to fake having a weapon, she's going to need something more convincing.

She halts, glancing at the door we came through and then looking at the top of the 3-D printer. "Boost me up," she whispers. "Quick."

I crouch to make a stirrup out of my hands, and she sets her foot in it. Then I straighten my legs and shove her upward.

Cleo grabs the top and pulls herself the rest of the way, and I dust my hands off, looking up and readying myself for the climb. *Earth strength, don't fail me now.*

I jump, straining up to grab at the edge of the machine,

which quietly hums to itself, unaware of my struggles. The edge is smooth, and I'm white-knuckled as I try to drag myself up the unforgiving surface with the strength in my hands alone. Why isn't Cleo helping me? I can't even see her up there.

The back of my neck is prickling, and I'm waiting for someone to come bursting through the door, weapon trained on me. Then with one more kick I'm moving, and I scramble up to flop onto the top of the printer, breathing hard. Below me, the machinery hums away.

And I don't know why, but that's the moment I realize I left our helmets by the ventilation pipes. If they work that out—if they have a way to flush this room . . .

I look around for Cleo, who's at the other end of the huge machine, reaching for a big box that sits on a high shelf. Her whole arm is extended, fingers straining, and as I watch, she manages to grab the box, pulling it toward herself.

Then it tips off the edge of the shelf, the contents beginning to spill, and I flinch—what was that and did we need it? But no, no we didn't. Cleo's fiendish.

With a series of clatters and pings, a box of ball bearings goes spilling across the floor of the workshop. They bounce like raindrops hitting the pavement, rolling into every corner, then ricocheting off whatever surface they hit and starting all over again. It's going to be *very* hard for our pursuers to move around the workshop.

Then, as I pull myself up to my hands and knees to get a better view of the impending carnage, Cleo unclips our tiny drone from her suit. She flips it over to inspect the bottom and opens its hatch to find the delivery net inside. I've seen these deliver takeout food before, but what . . . ?

She pulls the putty gun—is that what it is?—out of her belt, and jams it into the net. Then she flips her eyepiece into place and she waits. So I wait too. I have no idea what she's doing, but I know better than to interrupt a diabolical genius at work, and that's clearly what I'm witnessing.

Her red hair's falling around her face, and there's a smear of dirt on the fair skin of her cheek that I want to brush away. I can't help it—I let my gaze trace her profile, the curve of her lips, the graceful lines of her neck, the set of her jaw.

This girl is really something—beautiful, yes, but so much more. She's fierce.

How did I not notice before? I mean, I noticed *her*, but how did I ever think she was scared, or vulnerable?

She's fascinating, and I don't want to look away.

I said I'd help her get back to Earth, and of course I will, but I hope I can convince her to stay. Hers is the kind of ingenuity Mars needs. That GravesUP needs. And maybe there's something in her that *I* need.

A man comes bursting through the door—he's big, heavily built, with a nose that's been broken one too many times. This is one of the two guys we glimpsed in the corridor, right before we hid in the closet. He looks like a boxer, and his scowl says he's spoiling for a fight.

The Boxer makes it two steps into the room, and then hits the ball bearings and goes flying—he's actually horizontal in the air for a second, before he crashes down with a grunt of pain. Immediately he starts to push up, even angrier than before.

That's when Cleo flicks a switch on the putty gun and launches the drone, a stream of something trailing after it. And oh . . . *oh*. It's not putty.

It's expanding foam, the kind they use for emergency repairs.

The drone makes a pass over the Boxer like a tiny fighter jet dropping bombs, and as the pearls of foam hit him, they instantly start to grow, wrapping around his limbs and body and hardening in place. He has the presence of mind to cup a hand over his face and preserve his airways, but in less than three seconds, he's immobilized.

Two down, five to go, and five and a half hours left until this place explodes.

Cleo's actually *grinning* as she slides down the far side of the printer, hits the floor silently, and gestures for me to follow.

This girl is a *badass*.

Without a word, we head for the door on the far side of the workshop, and I slip through it after her, honestly just waiting to see what she's going to do next.

She's *really* something.

13.

CLEO

5 HOURS, 30 MINUTES REMAINING

I'M SO, SO STUPID.

Cleo, you might ask. *Aren't you being a little harsh? You're operating under a lot of pressure here. What about a little self-forgiveness?*

I wish the pressure was why I didn't take him to my hideout, which would have been a lot safer than where we are now.

I led him all the way here, I got us *shot at*, and then I chickened out. I turned right, into the workshop, instead of left into the repair center.

All we had to do was head *one* room into the repair center, and we'd have been through an emergency supplies closet and into one of my favorite nests.

But I didn't want him to know I had it. I didn't want him to ask how I knew it was there. I didn't want to see the slowly dawning light in his eyes as he looked around at the blanket, the hoarded food, and realized that this was where I slept. That the reason I didn't want to go to my quarters to grab my stuff is that I don't *have* any stuff. Or any official quarters.

I wasn't ready for him to realize I'm a hitcher.

Now I yank Hunter into the chief engineer's office and turn to lock the door behind us. Together we duck behind her desk and jam ourselves underneath it, hiding out under the overhang.

We're pressed together, shoulder to shoulder, and I can feel how hard he's breathing. But he's grinning, with the freaked-out adrenaline of someone who's just survived a chase.

"Remind me not to piss you off," he whispers, shaking his head.

"Congratulations on surviving your first time getting shot at," I murmur in reply.

"Expanding foam? You just thought of that on the fly?"

I make myself shrug, though my heart's still hammering too. "I can do better."

Probably best not to admit it was inspired by the packing foam we used to smuggle me up here. I hope that guy gets even more claustrophobic than I did.

"I don't doubt you." He laughs softly. "You think they're going to bill us for all this damage? So far we've flooded a classroom, and I don't know how many tools they'll break trying to get that stuff off him."

"A lot. The foam's for emergency repairs. It's pretty tough."

Hunter just laughs again and buries his face in his hands, pulling himself together. He's coping pretty well, considering how sheltered his life must usually be.

"Anyway," I continue. "You can afford it. Probably hold off on calculating the total until we see what else we manage to pull off. Two down, five to go."

"Maybe fewer, if we can spread them out enough to isolate one. We only need one to use their handprint on a rover."

"Right. We shouldn't stay here for too long. We have work to do."

That's enough to turn Hunter serious. "And now we have to work around their cameras. They wouldn't have been using them before—why look at surveillance when there's nothing to see? They thought the place had been evacuated."

"Mmhmm. Now I'm assuming they'll be taking an interest. Can you—" I wave a hand. "Hack them?"

Hunter tilts his head to one side, probably running through some mental list of things he knows about software systems and cameras. Does he keep the entire Graves system architecture in his head? I'm beginning to think so. And then he grimaces. "I don't see how. There's no single point of failure, it's like a parallel circuit. Take one down, and the others pick up the load."

"Damn."

"Yeah, sorry, it's well designed." His warm brown skin has gone a little paler. "Are we trapped in this office?"

"Nah, don't worry, they're not everywhere. This place is on a budget, remember. We can get around the camera placements."

What I don't say is that I have plenty of experience at that.

I don't want my presence recorded any more than I can help it. For sure, I don't want to be seen going into or out of any of my hideouts.

"You," says Hunter, "are an incredibly useful person to have around."

I fan myself. "Oh, stop. I bet you say that to all the girls."

He snorts. "Yeah, women love to be told they're useful. That one always works." Then, pausing to consider it: "Actually, I guess it's better than the alternative."

My own laugh bubbles up. "You have no experience complimenting girls, do you? I bet you don't have to. You just stand there being you, and they try to climb you."

Hunter bites his lip. "Well, I . . . uh . . ."

I rest my chin on my hand and inspect him. "Do go on."

"It doesn't sound great when you put it like that," he admits. "Which nobody else ever does."

He runs a hand through his hair, and I can't help following the movement. His borrowed T-shirt is smudged with reddish-gray Martian dust from the vent pipes. His hair's askew, his green eyes alive. He's still breathing hard, and I can see the pulse at his throat as he tips his head back and closes his eyes for a moment, lashes lowering.

He's so much more human now than when I first met him. I'm not sure that's a good thing.

Then he opens his eyes and tilts his gaze sideways in the same moment and catches me staring at him.

My own gaze widens as I scramble for an excuse. I expect

him to laugh, or tease me, or preen like a guy who's used to the staring and has somehow pulled me into the same net that catches all the rest of them.

But he doesn't. He just turns his head and studies me in return, his gaze shifting ever so slightly.

For a moment, the rest of it falls away, and I'm absorbed in the green of his eyes, the way the light catches them. In the fleck of dust that's caught on one of his eyelashes. In the strands of dark brown hair that dip over his forehead, and in the strong lines of his brows.

Our breathing slows and syncs. I'm suddenly acutely aware of the places our bodies touch. And then slowly, so slowly, he lifts a hand, and gently brushes my hair back behind my ear. His touch is feather-light, and sparks zip through me, my skin tingling in the wake of his fingertips.

My mouth is dry and I can't remember how to move away. I don't think I want to. Whatever I was expecting from Hunter Graves, it wasn't a moment like this.

His lips curve to a faint smile, a hint of a dimple showing in one cheek. "Hi," he murmurs, almost inaudible.

I reach deep inside myself for some sense of self-preservation. I *cannot* be enjoying this. My stomach is *not* fluttering. And no tingling is happening anywhere. *Cleo, get it together!*

There are a thousand reasons I can't: who he is, who *I* am, where we are, the mercenaries hunting for us. We're both riding high on adrenaline, and our judgment is terrible right now. Right?

"We should concentrate," I whisper unwillingly. "People are trying to kill us."

"I can do more than one thing at once," he whispers in reply, and I can't tear my gaze away from his mouth. But he's waiting. He's letting me choose. He could lean in so easily, close that last small distance between us, and find my lips with his. He could set us both on fire.

Instead, this boy who has everything holds himself back, restrained by nothing but his own willingness to let me be the one who decides. It's a kind of power that sends a shiver through me.

The little Cleo in my head, who hasn't been kissed in nearly a year, is doing backflips. *Get in there, girl!* she's screaming. *You know he knows how!*

But I have to keep a cool head. I have to find a way out of this—I have to live. And that means that if it comes down to it, I have to be prepared to trade him for my freedom. Nobody else is here for me. I have to take care of myself.

I really hope I don't have to hand him over, though.

There's another option, a part of me whispers. *With someone like Hunter, you could stop running, start living.*

Sparks skitter along my skin, all the way from the back of my neck to my fingertips, as I imagine that future. But I've learned what happens when I put my fate in someone else's hands.

I let out a slow breath and lean back a fraction. That's all it takes—he eases back too and he shoots me a quick, easy grin that tells me everything's fine. And I shove down my disappointment, biting the inside of my cheek to try to ground myself. He might be many things—a capitalist billionaire who grinds the poor beneath his boots, for example—but he doesn't pressure a girl, so I guess he's got that going for him.

"So," he says quietly. "I guess at some point we have to stop hiding under this desk."

"Sooner than later," I agree, amazed at how even my voice sounds. "We should keep going, while two of them are out of commission."

But I don't get any further than that, because that's when the PA system crackles to life.

14.

HUNTER

5 HOURS, 25 MINUTES REMAINING

***GREETINGS,* SAYS A VOICE** from near the ceiling. I startle, banging my head against the underside of the desk, and hiss a curse as I reach up to check if I'm bleeding. Beside me, Cleo's gone perfectly still. *I assume you have access to a headset,* the voice continues. *Please set it to channel four. I'd like to have a conversation.*

I'm not sure if my head's spinning from the whack I just gave it, or the trance Cleo had me in a moment ago.

She looks just as shaken, but after a moment she blinks, and then twists so she can snake an arm up onto the desk, grab the chief engineer's headset, and pull it down. I hold my hand out for it, and she scowls and puts it on over her own ear.

This would be a lot easier if either of us was a follower.

I lean in to try to hear the conversation, but don't want to touch my face against hers after the moment we just had—then she makes an annoyed sound and yanks me closer, so I let myself press my cheek to hers.

She taps the headband to bring up a display that only she can see, then swipes her finger through the air, presumably choosing channel 4. A voice issues from the headset immediately, broadcasting on a loop, I guess.

. . . Let us know when you're receiving. Repeat, once you're ready to talk, let us know—

"What do you want?" Cleo demands. She sounds different—she's made her voice lower, rougher, older than it is. It's a smart move. I wouldn't have thought of it.

We want to find a resolution that works for all of us, says the voice. It's low, authoritative.

"The Pirate," Cleo whispers, her mic off. That would be my guess too—this voice sounds like it belongs to the leader we saw on the bridge. The guy with the eye patch.

How did you get left behind? he asks, his tone light, curious.

"I was in bed with your mom," Cleo drawls. "I didn't hear the evac alarm over the sound of her screaming."

My gaze snaps up, but there's a snort of static over the channel, and I realize he's laughing. *Okay,* he says slowly. *This I can work with. Let me start by apologizing for the fact that we shot at you.*

"It sure didn't feel like the start of a beautiful friendship," Cleo agrees, her casual tone at odds with the tension in her expression.

Fair. We didn't actually come here to kill anyone. That's why we were so careful to evacuate the station before we began.

"So why *did* you come here?" Cleo asks without missing a

beat. Her fingers are drumming on her knee, and I trace the path of her tattoo up her forearm, flowers and vines curling around each other.

My mind flicks back to the files I caught them trawling through when I was in the greenhouse, watching them opening the UN Central Registers one by one. We can't ask about those specifically—no value in telling them what we know.

It doesn't matter why we're here, the Pirate says. *What matters is that you are too. Here's my offer: Come join us, and we'll take you with us when we're done.*

Now it's Cleo's turn to laugh. "And then you'll set us free, trusting in our goodwill and our silence?"

Not immediately, no, he admits. *But this is your best option, I promise you that. Later, we'll release you. Trust me when I tell you that you don't want to be here at the end of this. As I said, we didn't come here to kill anybody. We're not that kind of criminal.*

"And yet you brought guns."

Well, he says, and I can hear the shrug. *Other people could be that kind of criminal.*

"I thought there wasn't supposed to be anybody here," Cleo presses. Do they teach debate at engineering school?

The Pirate lets out an audible sigh. *I think we've all learned a lot today about how plans don't always unfold the way we want them to.*

Cleo reaches up to tap her headband again, muting the line. "We can't trust him," she murmurs.

"Not for a minute," I agree. "But I'm interested to hear what he says. The more we get him to talk, the better." I can practically hear my mother's voice in my ear. *Mouth shut, ears open. Learn more than you share.*

Cleo brings the headset back online. "I'm wondering why you'd take us with you," she says. "Why you wouldn't just shoot us, as soon as you see us. What's in it for you, to keep us alive? And do *not* say you prefer a clean conscience."

All right, I won't, the Pirate replies. *For a start, I'd like to know how to extract my team member from the classroom you managed to electrify.*

"We're not useful once you know that," Cleo points out.

No, he agrees. *And we'll figure out how to get her out by ourselves, eventually. I'm trying to demonstrate a little goodwill here, by giving you an opportunity to demonstrate yours.*

"Hey," Cleo replies, grinning. "You know who else is full of goodwill toward me?"

Again, I hear the Pirate's sigh. *Let me guess. My mother.*

She's got him on the back foot, half charmed, half annoyed. I'm fascinated by her savvy, her quick instincts. It's clear she knows how to talk to people like him—a mix of smarts and sass, not pushing too hard, but certainly not giving way.

I'm guessing she learned to do this when she was on the run from the debt collectors. I can't imagine what that was like, but it's made her tough in ways that are different from the ones I'm used to.

She's been through so much, and it makes her prickly, that much I can tell. It brings her shields up in moments like the one we just had. If she'd leaned forward even a millimeter, we'd have kissed. My chest tightens just thinking about it.

Is it stupid to be thinking about kissing Cleo with five mercenaries still out there hunting for us? Sure. It might also be the last chance I get.

I only realize Cleo's ended the call when she pulls the headset off.

"All done?" I ask, blinking back to the problem at hand.

"It never would have worked out between us," she replies with a shrug.

I can't help it. I wink and gesture at my dusty, sweaty self. "How could it, when you've got all this right here in front of you?"

Cleo rolls her eyes. "Let's find a better place to shack up, just in case someone comes to visit. And I think we'd better get started on some gifts for the neighbors."

4 HOURS, 36 MINUTES REMAINING

About forty-five minutes later, I'm laying out five headsets on a table in a corner of the cafeteria. The room's gone into power-saving mode for some reason, the lights dimmed, and even if someone walks straight through here—and I'm hoping they will pretty soon—they're unlikely to notice them sitting there.

Half the other tables were littered with food and trays when we came in, but Cleo hurriedly cleared them away before she disappeared. That'll be relevant in a minute, with any luck.

I'm listening for any news on the headset we stole from the

chief engineer's office, keeping an eye on the door to the corridor outside as I get my little speaker connected to a battery and check the settings on the headsets. If this works, it's going to be the most obnoxious thing I've ever done, and I once sold a guy his own company back for twice the price, after renaming it in honor of my childhood cat.

I'm straining to hear footsteps and trying to keep my hands from shaking as I bring up the display on the next headset and swipe through to channel 4. I can't afford to miss the only warning I'll have when company arrives.

There are cameras here in the cafeteria, but a pair of wire clippers took care of their connection in just a few seconds. They're not the sort of thing you carefully protect against sabotage when you build a peaceful base.

We had to take out a bunch of others as well, as diversions, so our friends wouldn't come right here, and that chewed up precious minutes. If we pull this off, though, it'll be worth it. We're still about four and a half hours from blastoff.

Then I hear the sound I've been waiting for, and my heart kicks up a notch. I slip around to the far side of the table I'm working at, sinking down to crouch behind it as one of the mercs strides into the cafeteria, pausing to look around at the half-lit room, the dozens of tables stretching out in neat rows. I see his shoulders slump as he thinks about having to search around and behind and between every one of them.

Then Cleo's voice comes from the kitchen, and I think he and I both stop breathing.

"I think this is going to work," she calls. "Let me take a look."

The merc is a Nordic blond, sharp-featured and muscular. He's the remaining member of the pair we saw patrolling the corridor—the Boxer was the other.

This is the kind of guy who stirs an instinct in the back of your mind telling you to stay very, very far away from him. Telling you that he'll hurt you without even thinking about it. He wears a pressure suit like we do, and like us, he's peeled it down halfway, the arms tied around his waist. His upper half is in a tight black T-shirt that was presumably designed to show off biceps the size of my head, and it's getting the job done admirably.

I would very much prefer not to go anywhere near him if I can avoid it. You just know he gets up at dawn, takes a cold shower, and then does chin-ups before breakfast. One-handed.

He draws his gun, stalking toward the kitchen, and I silently set down my headsets and speakers, preparing to move.

Mr. Chin-Up creeps past the serving counter and makes it to the entrance, disappearing into the kitchen. With a deep, steadying breath, I rise to my feet to sneak after him.

"Are you listening?" Cleo calls. "And hey, we should get more snacks while we're here."

On silent feet I jog across to the kitchen, making it to the entrance, my mouth dry. Will they have knives in there? Will I have time to grab one if I have to?

The kitchen is a long, narrow space, crowded with pots and pans, bunches of herbs and vegetables picked from the greenhouse, and big pots still sitting on the stove where the cooks abandoned them during the evacuation.

Mr. Chin-Up is halfway down the room, gun up and out, standing perfectly still as he listens. Then there's a faint sound from the huge walk-in freezer, whose door stands ajar, its interior as disorganized as the rest of the kitchen. It's not much—just a quiet, almost muffled click, as if someone's brushed against one of the walls.

He's across the kitchen in three long strides and slipping through that gap in the door.

That's when I really move, breaking into a run. But I've screwed up Mars gravity again, and I slam way too hard into the freezer door, sending a bolt of pain through my shoulder.

Cleo comes scrambling down from the high shelf where she was hiding. She drops the remote control she's holding, and as I push the long door handle closed, she's ready to slip a zip tie around it, securing it against the shelving units next to it. Then she adds another for good measure and carefully hangs a cleaning cloth over the handle, so that on a quick inspection, the fact that it's secured shut will be hidden.

There's silence from inside, where Mr. Chin-Up is no doubt discovering that his only company is a small cleaning robot, trying helplessly to bang its way free of the maze of frozen food we built for it. The thick insulation of the freezer walls blocks all sound, but the recording is probably still playing Cleo's voice at him, and it'll have progressed to a warning: *Pull up your pressure suit now, for protection against the cold. You might be here for a while.*

Cleo steps back, her hands clapped over her mouth to stifle a giggle. "I can't believe that worked," she manages. And then:

"Oh, you're kidding." She points, and when I follow the line of her finger, I see the warning sign beside the zip-tied door.

Please check for staff inside the freezer before closing, every time. Safety first!

And now I'm laughing too—I'm laughing too hard, with the heady relief of not having to fight a terrifying muscle man with a kitchen knife. "I'm a Graves," I manage with a shrug. "Rule-breaking's always been our thing."

I can't remember the last time I laughed like this—with the wild weakness that comes from having braved something terrifying and somehow survived it. Or, wait . . . I can, actually.

I was about twelve, and I was with my sister. We'd snuck into our mother's conference room before a board meeting, and then heard the board members all arriving early. Our choices were to dive under the table, or show ourselves and catch hell for being in a room full of classified papers. We dove under the table.

We stayed put for the whole two hours, desperately trying not to make a noise, and at one point Marguerite nearly suffocated me, trying to stop me from sneezing. If our mother had caught us down there, we'd have been skinned alive.

When the last of them left, we collapsed in laughter, clinging to each other, and every time one of us managed to get it under control, we'd make eye contact and start again. It's one of the last memories I have of us together, before it all . . . well, went how it went.

Cleo presses a hand to her mouth again, but doesn't really manage to chase away the laughter. "We should keep moving," she says. "He's going to spend a minute trying to get out, before he abandons his dignity and radios for help. Assuming he can get a signal through the freezer insulation, but let's say he can, just in case. Did you get the headsets prepped?"

"You get the food ready. I'll turn it on," I reply, snagging a muffin on my way out of the kitchen. Back at my nest of headsets, I carefully lift them off the table and set them underneath, where they're even better concealed. Then I check each of them is tuned to one of the base's communication channels, of which there are five.

And then I turn on the speaker.

Immediately my own headset is filled with the song now broadcasting on all five channels, the perky tones of Victoriana Lu earworming their way straight into my head.

Gonna blast into space, baby!

Gonna hit third base, baby!

Gotta love this face, baby!

Rocket to the moon, yeah!

I rip my headset off, wincing. My pain is worth it, though. Everyone on this base with a headset just got hit with the same song. And it's on loop. Which means that until they find my little setup, our friends just lost their comms.

That should help even the odds.

Over near the entrance to the kitchen, Cleo is carefully laying out the remains of a meal for six people—dirty plates, half-eaten food, half-finished drinks, and a big, tempting bowl of fresh fruit in the middle of the table. Spacers *love* fresh fruit and vegetables—even with the greenhouse here, they're not that easy to come by.

"I should have eaten some," I say, casting an eye over her offering. "Is that an apricot? We only had apples on the freighter out here, it was inhuman."

She fixes me with an unreadable look, but turns out that's fine, because she kindly translates a moment later. "Do you know what an apple costs?" she asks. "I can count on one hand the number of times I've eaten one in my *life*. And I've *never* had an apricot."

"But they—" I have no idea where I'm heading with that, because talking about my usual breakfast of fruit that some lackey has carefully cut into the shapes of flowers would probably get me punched. Thankfully she cuts me off.

"They're prepped, and they're not for us."

"Wipe your hands off," I remind her.

"On your face," she mutters, which immediately gets Victoriana singing in my head again. *Gotta love this face, baby!*

I decide not to share the line out loud.

"All ready," she continues, looking up. "Headsets done?"

"You wanna hear? We could have a sing-along. It's catchy stuff."

She snickers, and the grin makes her eyes sparkle. She really has a great smile, and it feels good to earn a laugh from her. "I will kill you," she threatens. "And if you even try singing to me about third base—"

"Please, Cleo." I frown in mock disapproval. "We're in the

middle of trying to overcome a hostile mercenary force. I hardly think now is the time for—"

And then it's her turn to interrupt me, whacking me on the arm. "Shut up, rich boy. Let's keep moving. We have more to do."

15.

CLEO

4 HOURS, 20 MINUTES REMAINING

HUNTER GETS THIS LITTLE line between his eyebrows when he concentrates, and I can't stop taking peeks at it.

We're making our way through the long, narrow reclamation room that runs behind the kitchens, past the greenhouse, and ends up at the communal showers. Those are the three heavy water uses on the base, so it makes sense to have them side by side.

It's really just a passageway—I can stretch out my arms on either side and touch the walls—and it's crammed with tanks and tubes we have to squeeze past and step over. The dehumidifiers that are all over the base work nonstop in here, and still don't manage to keep up. The warm, steamy air fills my lungs, and my face beads with sweat.

Right now, Hunter's carefully untangling a nest of cables to make a gap big enough to squeeze through—I've been along here before, but he's so much broader than me.

It's only luck that I happen to glance back the way we came.

It's nearly dark in here—there's just a low strip of emergency lighting along the floor—and at first I'm not sure whether something moved near the entrance, or whether it was a burst of steam floating through a beam of light.

Then that hint of movement resolves into a hand lifting, and the light glints off a gun, and without thinking I throw myself back at Hunter, crash-tackling him to the ground. It only works because he's still not used to the gravity, and he's thrown off-balance easily enough that my weight will do it.

In the same instant there's a deafening sound that echoes up and down the narrow room, and sparks fly off a nearby water tank.

Without a word the two of us scramble away, staying low, ripping cables out of our way. Hunter bulldozes a path for us and I'm right on his tail, flinching as there's another *BANG* behind us.

We come up on two doors, one leading forward to the showers, the other an access port leading out into the main hallway. Hunter doesn't know where he is, and picks the hallway door, shoving it open and throwing himself through it.

I'm right behind him, hitting the floor and rolling to the side in case a bullet follows me out.

"This way," I hiss, heading straight across the hall to the room that serves as a movie theater. It used to be a records room, and I knew it a lot better then. I yank open the door and usher him through, then close it behind us silently.

There's a huge screen taking up most of the wall to our left—when they put it up, they blocked an entrance I used to use to slip in and out of a back passageway—and to our right they've created a series of risers, and set out chairs facing the screen. There's an abandoned pair of augment glasses on each seat, and the smell of popcorn lingers in the air. This place will probably smell of popcorn forever.

It's almost pitch-dark in here, but there are little guidance lights stuck to the edge of each of the steps, and they provide just enough of a hint to see by, especially if you know the place.

If our stalker is just a few steps behind us, they'll come out from the access passage into an empty hallway, and not know which way we went. But in case our luck doesn't fall that way, I hurry up the steps toward the back of the room, then duck down to crawl along behind a row of chairs, Hunter on my tail.

A moment later the door opens, letting in a stream of brighter light from the hallway, and both of us freeze in place. I can see Sabrina silhouetted in the doorway, another slighter figure behind her. I can *feel* the adrenaline kick through my body as it returns to flight mode on pure instinct. I've run from Sabrina before. I know what she's capable of.

She has a tablet in one hand and she pauses in the doorway as she glances down at it. The faintest hint of music escapes the headsets they're wearing, and I hear the tinny tones of Victoriana Lu from a distance. *Gonna blast into space, baby!*

She smacks at the panel beside the door where the light switches are, then smacks at it again. Then I hear her voice: "Won't turn on. Leave the door open."

I can hear the soft, frustrated hum of the door trying to automatically close itself. Then Sabrina speaks again.

"It's a fucking cinema. The door won't stay open. How does this job keep finding new ways to screw me?"

Her companion's voice comes then, a woman crooning a singsong threat that makes my skin crawl. "We're better in the dark than you are, little mice."

Sabrina lets the door slide closed behind them and then hits the control panel, and the little guidance lights are gone.

The room's plunged into darkness, and they begin to stalk forward. I can only tell where they are by the sound of their headsets, and I reach out in the blackness for Hunter.

I find his shoulder, and when I pull him toward me, he comes willingly. I run a hand up his warm arm to find his shoulder, then curve it around the back of his neck, so I can pull his ear in close to my mouth. I breathe my words into his ear, lips brushing his skin. "Turn off your headset."

If I can hear their music, they'll be able to hear ours. Right now, I'm the only person in the room without Victoriana Lu blasting in my ear. But if either of them thinks to turn their music down, they'll be able to zero in on Hunter.

I feel him obey, rather than see him—his weight shifts slightly as he reaches up to the other side of his head, feeling for the switch and pressing on it.

They're coming closer. The buzzing sound of the music is halfway up the steps to us now.

Let's count down to a launch for two,

Let's blast off, baby, me and you-ouuu!

With a gentle push, I send Hunter crawling along the row of chairs again, moving toward the other end. Maybe we can circle around and try for the access door now hidden behind the screen. If it's still there.

I catch a flicker of light at the other end of the row as Sabrina's tablet comes to life for a moment, and glimpse her face as she looks down at it. What's she doing? She'll lose her night vision.

Hunter reaches the end of the row and pauses in the dark, uncertain. He must be completely lost. I reach out to rest a hand on his back, and then with agonizing slowness, I squeeze between him and the row of chairs so I can take the lead.

How am I going to get him behind the screen when he can't see a thing?

I take his hands to pull him to his feet, and he comes up silently, then stands unmoving. I weave my fingers through his for a moment and squeeze. A silent *trust me*. He squeezes back.

Slowly, my ears straining for the faint sound of music, I turn away from him. Then I take his hands and settle them at my waist—they curve around the narrowest point, his fingertips pressing through the thin fabric of my tank. I can feel his breath on the back of my neck.

When I take a slow step forward, he follows, understanding. I can't imagine what it's like for him in this moment, in unfamiliar surroundings, in the pitch-black dark, knowing there are two people in this room who'll shoot us if they can find us.

I ease down another step, and together we start making our way toward the front of the room. A part of my brain is already setting to work a different problem: How did they find us? Did we miss a camera? Was it just a lucky guess? They seemed sure we were in here, though.

Another step down, and another, as we ease our way toward the screen. The ground levels off, and I stretch my hands out in front, feeling for the thick fabric of it, and then groping my way to the edge. Please, *please* let the access door still be there.

Another snatch of music tickles the edges of my hearing, maybe as one of them turns their head in the darkness.

Gotta love this face, baby!

The headset.

We took the chief engineer's headset, and they must have worked that out—they must have searched the areas around the workshop. And you can't just scan the whole base for anyone using a headset, but you *can* track a specific headset. If you know which one you're looking for.

That's what Sabrina's looking at on the tablet.

The huge screen is suspended from the ceiling, and I feel my way behind it with my hands on the wall, and Hunter's hands still around my waist, his body pressed close to mine. He doesn't pause, doesn't slow, doesn't even give me a what-the-hell squeeze. He just lets me steer.

My fingers find the fine seam where the door used to be, and I sweep slowly with my hands until I find the handle. They're going to hear when I open it, so we'll have just one chance.

I reach for where Hunter's hand rests at my waist and tap my fingers against it. First one, then two, then three. A countdown.

A quick squeeze lets me know he understands—or at least, I hope that's what he's saying.

I give him the countdown again: one, two, three.

On the third tap, I open the door and step through it, pulling him with me.

"There!" someone shouts, and a bullet pierces the screen, sending shuddering ripples through it.

I slam the door shut, turning in Hunter's arms and groping at his face in the darkness, until I find the headset tucked behind his ear. I rip if off, dropping it to the ground and stomping hard.

"Cleo?" he whispers, still holding me tight—it's just as black in here as it was out there.

"They were tracking it," I whisper back. "Keep hold of me. I know the way through here."

"Go," he says simply, hands tightening at my waist as I turn away.

It's not even an emergency hallway—it's just a gap between two sections of the base, no wider than my body in some places. They design the sections to seal off from each other, so a breach in one leaves the others intact, but nobody's meant to come through here. These passageways have been a useful place to camp out, or even to sleep. They're also free of obstacles, which means I can jog, my hands trailing along each wall, waiting until I feel the seam I'm looking for.

The floor dips as we pass underneath the ring corridor that circles the base, then climbs again. We move for nearly a minute in silence before we find the place I want, and Hunter presses into the back of me when I suddenly stop. I feel for the inside release I installed about a month ago, then flick open the door.

My eyes swim with tears as we step into the small storage room off the main shower facility, where they keep all the spare towels, the cleaning supplies.

Hunter follows me, and I hear his intake of breath behind me as we suddenly step into the light. It's not bright, but it's dazzling after so long in the dark.

His hands slide from where they rest at my waist to wrap around my middle, pulling me back against him. Now it's my turn to go where he steers, and I turn my head so I can press my cheek to his chest. I feel his heart thumping there, quick but steady. *Alive*, it says. *Alive, alive, alive.*

He's silent, and I fold an arm over his, so he doesn't let go. Just for a minute, I let myself lean on him. I let us share this moment of sheer relief that we got away, that we're together, that he's here and warm and strong and sharing the load of getting through this.

You could have left him, whispers a little voice. She's the one who looks out for me, mostly. *You would have been safer if you'd left him behind. But it didn't even occur to you.*

Shut up, I whisper back, in the silence of my head.

And then I pull myself together.

"They'll find a light source eventually," I say, my voice sounding loud, even though I'm only murmuring the words. "And then they might find the door behind the screen. We should keep moving."

"Right," he says, his voice low in my ear. But he doesn't let go for a moment longer. Then he uncurls his arms from around me and steps back. "Let's head to the greenhouse. We need the terminal there. If they're using the cameras, we need them too."

Four hours to go. *Tick, tock.*

16.

HUNTER

4 HOURS REMAINING

I SETTLE INTO MY old friend Susanna's chair in the greenhouse, and let out a slow, shaky breath as I log in to her daisy-adorned console. The door to the greenhouse is zip-tied shut, and we're confident we got here without the cameras clocking us.

I glance across as Cleo adjusts her headset. "You're *sure* that thing can't be traced?" I ask again.

"Positive," she replies. "I know you're the software guy, but this was a hardware fix. I modded it as a project a few months ago. Took out its locator chip—took me forever to pull it apart then put it back together again."

"And you did this why?"

She shrugs. "Let's say I have trust issues, I had some downtime, and I enjoy a challenge. And aren't we glad of that right now, huh?"

I can't help making a mental note of it—we should embed the locator function into the software so it can't be physically removed—but for now, it's the answer I want to hear.

We're not safe, but we're as safe as we're getting for the time being—if only my body would figure that out, and let me step down from this hyperalertness.

I'm still humming a jittery version of the Victoriana Lu song to myself as I open up the menus I want, starting the hunt for camera feeds.

A part of me is still back in the total blackness, Cleo warm and alive beneath my hands, that contact the only thing anchoring me to reality. How is it possible that I didn't know her a few hours ago?

If we'd met before now, we'd never have given each other a second look. Well, that's not true—I'd have looked twice at her no matter where I met her. She's beautiful, and I'd have known that even if I'd known nothing else.

But we're both guarded in our own ways, for our own reasons, and it shows up differently for each of us. I have more questions than answers about her—she knows parts of this station where nobody goes, and I can tell she's keeping more to herself than she tells.

We've both learned not to rely on anyone, because one way or another, they'll let you down or leave.

Just now, though, she had my life in her hands, and I let her hold it. In the dark we were one breath, one body. She held me as carefully as she holds her secrets.

I find a limited camera feed—we clipped a bunch of wires, so there aren't as many viewing options available as before—and start to flick through the screens.

I wonder what my mother and sister are doing right now. It's nearly lunchtime, so maybe they're getting ready to grab a bite and then take over a small country before cocktails or something.

It's so strange to think we're this close—physically—but they have no idea I'm here. I wonder what they'd do if they knew.

I wonder what they'll think if Cleo and I don't make it through this. If I'll be identified, and . . .

I nearly swipe past the view of the hallway outside the cafeteria, then catch my breath, leaning in to get a better look at a flicker of movement.

The Martian is strolling out of the cafeteria. There's a grace to the way he walks that I see a little of in Cleo, and in a few of the mercenaries—a comfort with this gravity that takes time to develop. He's holding something in his hand, and . . . holy shit, it's an apricot.

"Come on," I whisper. "Take a bite. Take a bite, you know you want fresh fruit."

"What's happening?" Cleo calls softly, from somewhere behind me.

"He's taking the bait," I breathe.

She's behind me a moment later, leaning in over my shoulder to watch with me. We stare together, silently willing him on as he lifts the piece of fruit to his mouth and then sinks his teeth into it. He's still chewing as he takes a second bite. And then, without warning, he sinks bonelessly to the floor, sprawling there with the apricot still in his hand.

"Yes!" I lean back in my chair, lifting both fists in the air and tipping my head back with a grin to watch Cleo dancing in a circle behind me, swinging a hand above her head like she's going to lasso the next guy we take down.

"That's four!" she crows.

Blue Braid's presumably still stuck on the table, the Boxer is wrapped in foam, Mr. Chin-Up is in the freezer, and the Martian will be unconscious for hours, if we got the dose right. He found the remains of that six-person feast we left out, and just like in the garage, he started snacking. Sabrina did say he's always eating, so we laid out that fresh fruit in the middle of the table as bait especially for him—a luxury that a Martian wouldn't be able to resist. And thanks to our raid on the infirmary supplies, he should be out for a long time.

"You know, I don't want to get ahead of myself," Cleo says slowly. "But . . ."

"We might not *definitely* die?" I finish for her.

She shoots me a grin I'd have flown to Mars just to see. "You never know."

17.

CLEO

3 HOURS, 55 MINUTES REMAINING

I WATCH HUNTER'S FINGERS fly over the keyboard, studying his hands as he lifts one to swipe away a display, grab a cookie, take a bite, get back to work. There's an ease to the way he does it—I can believe his family created these systems. He doesn't even seem to think about what he's doing. It's as natural as breathing to him because he grew up with this code as his playground. His family's DNA is in this stuff, and when he walks through it, he's at home.

"We need someone isolated," he says, eyes on the screen. "If we're going to force a rover out of them, this is the time. There are three of them left at large—the two who stalked us through the movie theater, and the Pirate. This is our best chance that one of them will end up on their own—to look for someone missing, or to help someone. Once they start solving problems, the odds will be against us again."

I need our one to be the Pirate, or the woman who was with

Sabrina in the cinema—because if it's Sabrina herself, she'll recognize me, and say my name, and then everything about who I am will start to unravel.

I'm by the tomato vines, picking the ripe ones as I scan the channels on my headset, waiting to see when the music in my ear is going to switch off. I'm deeply regretting Hunter's choice of music, because I am never, ever going to stop singing this song. *Curse you, Victoriana Lu.*

I bite down on another tomato, and look up to see that Hunter has paused his work and is watching me.

I shouldn't do this. It's such a bad idea. But even as I'm thinking that, I run my tongue over my upper lip, catching a stray drop of juice.

Hunter stares a beat too long before he remembers how to blink and goes back to work.

As he comes undone, Hunter Graves looks better and better—his ridiculous stolen T-shirt and his easy grin make me forget he's a billionaire. He's just Hunter, the guy who keeps sneaking cookies from the backpack, who tries to make me laugh when the tension threatens to overwhelm me. Who can tell when I need that.

Come on, Cleo. What are you doing? This is a guy you still might have to trade for your freedom. But the truth is, the longer this goes, the harder I'm finding it to imagine doing that.

Still, I can't forget that after this is over—if we make it through—we'll belong in two different worlds again.

For now, I lean back against the vines, allowing myself a moment to enjoy the view while he's concentrating.

And that's when the music stops. *Shit.*

I'm drawing breath to warn Hunter when a voice sounds in my ear, and my whole body locks in place.

Cleo, Cleo, Cleo. Now this is a pleasant surprise.

It's Sabrina. My throat tightens, and I can't even make myself breathe. My gaze snaps to Hunter, but he's lost in his work again, trusting me to listen on the headset. What do I do?

The question's barely formed in my mind when I start moving. It's not even a choice. I just find myself clearing my throat, waiting until Hunter's gaze flicks my way. "I'm going to hit the restroom," I say, my voice perfectly calm, perfectly even.

"I'll try not to finish all the cookies while you're gone," he replies. "No promises."

I turn away, walking along the trellis of tomato plants, reaching out to trail my fingertips along their green leaves. I walk across the little footbridge that crosses the fishpond, the ghostly silver tilapia swirling past beneath me with flicks of their fanlike tails.

Sabrina's still talking in my ear. *You came a long way to see me, babe. I didn't know we were that close, but I'm here for it.*

I have to say something, but my throat's so dry. I slip through the door to the tiny restroom and let it close behind me. Then I pull in a slow, deep breath, letting my lungs fill, my ribs expand. I center myself and wait until I know my voice will sound calm. And then I flick the transmit button and answer her.

"I didn't think you'd recognize me," I say, playing for time.

I caught your face for a second there before you snipped the wires on the cafeteria feed, Sabrina replies. *Took me a moment to place you, but sure I remember you. You were the one who got away.*

"Want me to apologize for ruining your perfect record?" I shoot back.

She laughs. *Hey, you know it was never personal. Anyway, you still have your kneecaps, and nobody from Gramercy is here. What the hell are* you *doing here?*

"Here at Pax, or here on Mars?"

Both. Either.

"Same answer, really," I reply, making my hands into fists, watching my knuckles turn white, channeling my tension there, so it doesn't sound in my voice. "Decided to treat myself to a vacation. You know how it is."

Oh, you know I do.

This is the moment. If I'm going to tell her who I'm with, if I'm going to talk about a deal, I have to at least hint at it. Show her the door's open. It's the smart thing to do. There are still three of them out there, they're armed, and we're on a clock—less than four hours left.

It's not time to make a deal yet, but it's time to give her a glimpse, show her I don't hate the idea.

"What about you?" I make myself say. "What's a nice girl like you doing in a place like this?"

There's a pause as she considers what to tell me, and then she offers her reply. *We're here for the registers. There are a whole lot of people on a list, folks who hitched up. Our job is to enter them in, make them legal.*

My heart stutters and nearly stops. What? *What?* Hunter did say they were looking at the registers. Could Sabrina be telling the truth? Holy shit, could the bad guys be the good guys?

You there, babe? Sabrina asks, when I don't reply.

"I'm here," I reply, trying not to stammer.

I'm thinking maybe we should talk about a situation where we stop shooting at you, you help us get our guys out of here? I can vouch for you. I knew you before, and I saw firsthand that you were smart. The boss won't hold a grudge. We could even add your name to the register, if you'd like the vacation to last forever.

I'm still scrambling for a coherent thought. Could this be real?

"Why?" I manage. "Why would *you* take a job like that?"

Sabrina laughs. *What, you don't think I'm an idealist who wants Mars for everyone? Some of the others are, actually. But we're all being paid.*

"By who?" I ask. "The hitchers you're doctoring the registers for are dead broke, or they wouldn't be hitching." I lean against the sink, staring at myself in the mirror. Brown eyes stare back at me, faint freckles standing out against skin that's gone pale with stress and exhaustion. My red hair hangs lank around my face, dull and gross after so much sweat, so many frantic action sequences.

True, not being paid by hitchers, Sabrina agrees. *Or not in cash. But some of them have valuable skills, and various corporations want them on payroll. Can't do* that, *unless they're on the register. Who else are you here with, babe? If they're as sweet as you, we can talk about getting them on the list.*

Oh, of course. She thinks there are more of us. The Martian probably reported in on the plates of staged leftovers he found in the cafeteria, before he ate his apricot and knocked himself out.

And suddenly there's bile in the back of my throat. Because there's only one other person with me, and he's not like me—or Sabrina—at all. I'm pretty sure Hunter would rather die here than do a deal with these people who are here to help hitchers—and I doubt they'd do a deal with him at all, not when they could sell him to the highest bidder.

Cleo, I'd much rather you were my teammate than my prisoner, Sabrina says, coaxing. *You know I don't hurt people for fun, girl. I showed you that back on Earth, in that club. It's all business, so let's find a way to make sure it isn't my business to do anything we both regret.*

I so badly want to believe her—to believe there's a way I can convince her to stop hunting me. I know she's not like some of the other bounty hunters and debt collectors back on Earth. She *didn't* hunt for fun. Which means that if there's not a business case for hurting me now, she won't.

Girl, Sabrina says, *you don't want to be left behind, trust me. This place won't be in good shape after we leave. It's going to look like an explosive systems failure, because that way nobody's ever going to say, "Huh, I wonder if anybody snuck in and hacked the registers before this disaster caused by poor maintenance."*

We're halfway through our eight hours.

It's time to make a move.

Why don't you give me something, for now, Sabrina suggests.

Let's keep the conversation going. We found the situation with the expanding foam in engineering, but another one of our guys is completely missing. Can you tell me about that?

I breathe out slowly, trying to stop my body from trembling. What do I do? Do I stick with Hunter? He said he'd help me get settled anywhere on Mars, but that offer will disappear once he finds out who I am.

Won't it?

Or I could side with Sabrina. I wouldn't have to rely on him. My life could change. I could get my name on the register. I could get real work, find a real place to settle. I could get a *new* name on the register.

I could stop running.

"Your missing guy isn't dead," I hear myself say. "He's just somewhere safe for now."

I mean, they'll figure that out anyway, now they've managed to unblock the radio channels. I'm barely even giving anything away.

Right?

I tear my gaze away from the scared girl in the mirror, and stumble out of the restroom. When I push open the door to the greenhouse a crack, I see Hunter there, still leaning over his console.

The light of the sunlamps plays over his features, and as I watch, he runs a hand through his dark, tousled hair, leaving it messier than before. He's watching something intently on the screen, grinning like a giant dork.

He's nothing like I thought he'd be.

I like him. I want to trust him.

If I open the door between me and Sabrina, I close the door between me and Hunter forever. But I'm not dumb enough to care about that, not when the life I've always wanted is on offer.

. . . Am I?

18.

HUNTER

3 HOURS, 44 MINUTES REMAINING

I LEAN BACK IN my chair once the screens start to blur together, gazing up at the ceiling where a passion fruit vine is snaking its way across the latticework. It reminds me of Cleo's tattoos, actually. The plants seem to find a way to cling to every little place they can—kind of like humans on the red planet, I guess.

What are the intruders looking for? They're still digging through the registers—well, what's left of the tech team is—but they're all over the place.

I let my gaze drop to the standard displays, scanning them idly. The navigation scan has Pax at the center of its circle, and a line that rotates slowly around the display, flicking past the nearby settlements one by one. I watch as they flash their names in turn. EURO W. EURO E. AFRO U. ARES TECH.

They're all agonizingly close, but totally oblivious. It feels like we're standing here in a crowd, but however loud we scream, nobody will hear us.

The scanning line sweeps around the navigation panel like a hand on a clock, and each one of them jumps to life for an instant as it passes. It's almost hypnotic, watching as each one flashes in turn.

And then there's a new ping.

I scramble forward in my chair, leaning down to get a better look at it. It's a dot halfway between us and Ares Tech, labeled UR-9999.

Hope jolts through me like a shot of adrenaline, like a flutter in my belly. I twist around to look for Cleo, who's hovering in the doorway. I can't even spit out words yet—I frantically wave her over, getting to my feet.

She kills whatever display she's looking at on the headset, jogging over toward me.

"There," I manage. "Something's coming. See that dot? It wasn't there before. We've got things much farther out—all the big stations. So if that just started showing up, it must be small. In this storm, it had to get close enough to be picked up."

"What does that mean?" she asks, staring down at the nav scan, watching the line sweep around the circle.

"It means it could be a rover. Someone from Ares could be out and about."

"It's not quite on course to have come from Ares," she points out, squinting at it. "Oh, but there's a crevasse it would have to go around, and . . ." She trails off, then lifts her gaze to me as hope dawns. "Hunter, you think we can get them on comms?"

"I think let's find out. The mercs have the main comms to the other bases blocked, but local stuff is on a different system. They couldn't block it, unless they wanted to block on-base comms. Pair your headset to the console, hail them."

She swipes up her headset's menu—only visible to her, as the one using it—but her fingers dance in the air, and a moment later I accept the request at Susanna's station. Cleo hands me the headset, fumbling a little to get it off her temples. "You do it."

I don't argue, but just slip on the headset, still warm from where it rested against her skin. And then I send a ping to UR-9999.

Time drags out, every second stretching into a lifetime, and I force myself to count slowly. I've reached fifteen when it pings us back, and the screen lights up.

"Holy shit," Cleo whispers, and leans down to rest her hands on my shoulders, pressing her ear to mine to listen in.

I draw in a shaky breath and speak. "UR-9999, this is Pax Station hailing, do you read?"

There's a pause, and then a startled voice, crackling with static. *Pax Station, this is rover. What the hell are you doing there?*

Relief rushes through me like a river. I want to laugh, I want to cry—I want to slide down and sit on the floor, or float up to the ceiling. I lift my hand to squeeze Cleo's, where she rests it on my shoulder. She squeezes back, hard.

"Rover, that's a long story, but we are incredibly glad to see you."

Cleo grips my hand even tighter suddenly, and I hear her

quick intake of breath behind me. I mute the line, turning my head to look up at her.

"They can't listen in on this, right?" she whispers.

"We're safe," I reply. "It's a secure line, one comms point to another. We're not on one of the five public channels, so they won't pick it up on a general sweep."

Pax Station, do you need assistance? Rover is asking. It's a woman, her voice flattened by the transmission, but I can still hear her surprise. *Our information was that the station is repressurizing after a bio vent, but the signal's been fritzy, so I got diverted by Ares Base to scan from close up. We thought the mess on the signal was the dust storm, but if you're alive in there, I'm assuming you do have pressure?*

"Rover, I confirm the alarm was a false signal," I reply, lifting my hand to rest it over Cleo's on my shoulder. "We're alive, but we are not okay. The station's been invaded by a hostile force. If you have enough battery to make it here, we could really use a pickup."

There's another pause, and this one draws out just a beat too long—long enough for my gut to clench in fear that the signal has dropped, or Rover thinks we're pranking her, or—

Holy shit, comes Rover's voice. *Say again? Pax has been invaded?*

"Confirm, invaded," I reply. "By an armed force. We don't know what they're here for, but they've discovered our presence and they're trying to kill us."

Holy shit, Rover says again, shock audible in her tone. *How many of you are there? I don't have a lot of room in here.*

"There're two of us," I reply. "We're holed up in the greenhouse right now, but we can move to meet you."

Okay, yes. This thing isn't designed for three, but if you can bring an auxiliary oxygen tank with you, we'll make it work. I'm a geologist, I'm not armed. I just happened to be in the area, so they asked me to—okay. I'm the one here, I have to do this. I'll have to pull up, get you on board, and then we run like hell.

"Agreed."

And I have to pick you up from a garage. I have to get inside an airlock before I can open up the rover and let you in.

"Understood," I reply, then toggle the mute button again. "Cleo, they came in on the east side. So it's safer on the other side, right?"

"That's right," Cleo whispers, lifting her head and looking over her shoulder, as though she can see through the walls, see where our enemies are right now. "She'll have to pull up on the west side, where the main garages are. I don't know how we can get there without being seen, though. It's a long way."

"If the alternative is staying here, we'll figure it out," I reply. Then, unmuting the channel: "Rover, we'll meet you at the west garages, do you know them? They're the main intake facility here, so I'm guessing they're marked on the outside."

Visibility's almost zero with this dust storm, Rover replies. *But I can lock on to the nav beacon.*

I punch a button to bring up the external display, and get a view of outside the base that's a hazy red, the camera lens half encrusted with red dust, the air beyond it filled with the kind of fog that the dust storm creates. Rover's right—visibility's terrible.

Just please be there, all right? Rover continues. *I don't want to meet these people. My ETA is forty-five minutes.*

"We'll be there," I promise.

Okay. Going silent now. Rover out.

The faint hiss of static on the line dies away, and for a long moment, neither of us moves. Then I let out a slow breath and let my head fall back. "Did that just happen?"

"That just happened," Cleo whispers. "The cavalry's coming. Someone's going to freaking rescue us."

Slowly, the realization that this is real is trickling through me, bringing me to life one degree at a time. There's a way out of this.

There's a way out of this.

I push to my feet, turning and shoving my chair out of the way so I can reach for Cleo. She throws her arms around my neck, clinging to me, laughing as I whirl us in a circle, dizzy with relief and disbelief.

Then my foot catches the leg of my chair and I'm moving too fast in too little gravity to stop myself. Together we go staggering backward, Cleo's feet still not on the ground.

I let myself fall, arms around her, and land flat on my back, Cleo on top of me.

Her brown eyes are laughing, and her lips are right there, curved to a smile she can't hide. I want to kiss her so badly, and all I'd have to do is lift my head just a fraction. Then she'd lean down, and curl a hand around the back of my neck, her weight just right on top of me. And I'd—

Cleo rolls off me, landing on her back beside me, her hand

finding mine. She's still laughing, though she tries to stop. "You okay?"

"We're getting out of here," I tell her.

"We're getting out of here," she agrees, looking at me sidelong. And her warm brown eyes are dancing, and her red hair's falling around her face, and in this moment, I *wish* I could—

"Cleo," I hear myself say.

"Mmm?"

"Fair warning. If we live through this, I'm asking you out."

She gives me one of those smiles I'll do anything to earn. "If we live through this, I'm saying yes."

19.

CLEO

3 HOURS, 19 MINUTES REMAINING

THE HELL WITH SABRINA. I don't have to make the decision I was dreading, and I'm not going to.

I have many complicated and inconvenient feelings when it comes to Hunter Graves, but I have to believe that even if he's furious when he finds out what I am, he won't screw me. I have to believe he's not that guy. That the boy who followed me in the dark with total trust, who waited patiently as I debated whether to kiss him, and gracefully accepted my answer—I have to believe I can trust him.

In the end, I have to trust *someone* to see me as a person—either Hunter, or Sabrina and her boss. And I choose Hunter. The two of us fit together. We're both alone. We both got left behind by the people who were supposed to love us. We both had to fend for ourselves. And we've done that, together.

Also, Hunter's never threatened to break my kneecaps in a Jerhattan alleyway.

"The alarm should go off in about five minutes," Hunter says, looking up from where he's been carefully sawing through a pipe near the water recyclers. "There's plenty of vapor already escaping, and once it gets more than the humidifiers can take, they'll start screaming for help."

That alarm will be the first in a glorious sequence of events that are about to unfold, all hastily assembled in the last fifteen minutes. It helped that we were already knee-deep in plans for wreaking havoc before Rover showed up.

One of our enemies will have to come check what's setting off the alarm—maybe even two, if they're starting to get wary about moving around alone.

In the meantime, the two of us are going to pull on our suits and EVA across the *outside* of the base to reach the garage where our freaked-out geologist will meet us. Can't be caught on-camera if we're not inside.

Hunter's never done anything like this before—sure, he's done the training, but he's never actually been out where a suit is all that sits between him and sudden, icy death. I'm not the world's most experienced teacher, but I've paid a hell of a lot of attention to this particular area since I arrived—spying on safety briefings, watching the maintenance teams as they suit up—and I'll be doing my best to guide him.

We hustle back to the greenhouse to start suiting up properly, working our pressure suits up our bodies. "Do you know much about the Ares Base?" I ask, picking up my helmet and studying the seal for any damage, and then moving on to his, which I inspect just as carefully.

I never paid much attention to Ares Tech—I know they're small, and for sure too small for me to hide there, so I was interested in scamming a ride to a bigger station.

"Not much," Hunter replies. "They're a mining operation, minimal staff. I think they're tucked under the wing of either the Eastern or Western Euro group, I forget which."

That's how it works with all the groups who've claimed space on Mars. They're either big countries—the USA, Russia, China—or they're bunches of countries that have clubbed together, like the West African Union guys, or they're somewhere small that's put themselves under the protection of somewhere big, in exchange for a share of their profits.

The setup with the corporates is exactly the same. Only GravesUP is big enough to have its own claim. Smaller corps or countries tend to form uneasy alliances with each other to give themselves more power. The smallest corporations and countries are like little fish darting through a school of sharks, praying they can be useful to someone, and not just get eaten.

Ares is a little fish. If they've got a good mining claim, I'm guessing that's how they've scored protection from one of the big Euro groups. It's not real loyalty, though—it comes at a steep price.

Makes it all the more . . . something, that the Ares crew were the ones who came to investigate why the Pax signal seemed weird. The little guys were the ones who took the trouble.

Hunter straightens up from where he's busy hiding his backpack among the plants. He can't take it outside with us, and I guess he's hoping it'll somehow survive long enough for him to come back for it when all this is over. He carefully peels off the cuff he uses for his hacking and turns it over in the palm of his hand. It's got sharp enough edges that it could snag his suit, and so he tucks it into a pocket on his bag. We're both praying he doesn't need it again before this is done.

I settle my helmet into place and seal it at the neck, then hold out his—he bows his head and I carefully attach it, checking every seal twice.

Finally, we reach for our gloves. The suits are beautiful pieces of engineering, truly. There are heating elements woven through the inner layer to guard against the freeze-your-toes-off temperatures out there, an O_2 tank and power unit are strapped to each bank in a slim casing, and the helmets offer clear views of the red, red world outside.

Together, Hunter and I walk over to the airlock at the end of the greenhouse, and step inside. It's just big enough for the two of us—for sure not big enough for the rover, unfortunately. Still, there's about three and a quarter hours now until the base blows, and we're going to be *far* from here by then.

The door slides closed and seals behind us. I smack the exit button with my hand, and we wait in place as the pressure slowly changes around us, equalizing with the outside.

Hunter reaches over for my gloved hand, and I let him take it and pull me in against his side, though I'm careful not to let our helmets clash.

Then the sensor gives us the all-clear, and the outer doors swing open to reveal Mars waiting for us.

20.

HUNTER

3 HOURS, 15 MINUTES REMAINING

AS THE DOORS OPEN fully, a red world spreads out before us, shrouded in the haze of the dust storm.

To the east lie vast acres of solar arrays and the heads of the water pumps, which stand up above the fields of reflective black panels like giant scarecrows. They're just shadows against the murky sky, and the hair on the back of my neck stands up, like some part of my brain thinks they're giant predators that could come striding toward me at any moment.

It's a weird thought, and I shake it off as I follow Cleo out of the airlock to begin our walk around the outside of the base. My first time outside in a suit, and she's given me seventeen different kinds of safety lectures.

Coming to Mars was always about gain, for me. It was about snatching back opportunities Marguerite stole from me. About pushing my mother to acknowledge what I did back on Earth, however the execs try to cover it up. The determination that if my family wouldn't give me my birthright as a Graves, then I'd take it. Marguerite has spent years setting herself up to take over GravesUP one day. To be honest, I wouldn't be surprised if she picked that day herself and cut Mom's throat when she's ready. Metaphorically speaking. Probably.

I came here prepared to cut hers, prepared to play exactly the same game.

But I wasn't prepared for this place to be so beautiful.

The Martian regolith is different from the dirt on Earth, and the red dust is so much lighter than our dirt that it simply hangs suspended in the air like fog, concealing the plains of Arcadia Planitia behind its mystery.

Cleo's a few steps ahead of me, trailing her gloved hand along the side of the hab, leaving tracks in the dust there. Most of the base is buried under rock and dirt, but it has to surface in a few places, to let folks in and out. It does where we exited the greenhouse, and now we have a trek across the uneven ground that was laid on top of the base when it was built, before we reach the aboveground garage on the west side, where we'll meet Rover. It should take less than twenty minutes, if all goes well.

All I can hear inside my helmet is my own breathing, for the first fifteen minutes or so. Something about this place invites you to stay quiet, to soak it in. I didn't think it would hit me so hard, walking on the surface of another planet, but I feel incredibly small right now. As if even if I spoke, my voice would be so soft that this ancient place would just swallow it up.

I study Cleo's profile as she clambers over a rocky outcrop, then carefully slides down the other side. We're coming up on the entrance to the main western garage, the building jutting up out of the ground.

The dust is getting thicker all around us, more of it suspended in the air. When I look back—which means turning my whole body, since I can't turn the head of my pressure suit—I can't see where we came from anymore. The back of my neck prickles.

If we'd set off even a few minutes later, we wouldn't have been able to see where we were heading.

Cleo gestures toward the murky shape ahead of us, a new urgency in the quick cut of her hand, and I move a little faster to catch up with her. We're on a downward slope now, nearly there.

Right after I talked to Marguerite for the last time, I told my therapist that connections to other people just make you vulnerable. Just hurt, when they break. And that's true, but also, it's not.

If Cleo was hurt, or worse, something in me would break. Something about the enormity of this place makes it impossible to bullshit myself—I care about her. I want to know who she is, to learn her story. I want the time together that'll take.

But the thing about Cleo is that she hasn't *just* made me vulnerable, she's made me brave enough to do this too. How could I be anything else around a girl like this?

A couple of strides bring me up alongside her, and I reach for her hand, and she catches me in her peripheral vision and lets me take it. When we get into that rover, when we're speeding away from here, I'm going to—

A rock gives way under Cleo's foot, and she falls, her hand yanked from mine, the sudden release making her lose her balance completely. She hits the ground and rolls down the slope toward the garage, hands flying out to try to stop herself.

The power-and-air unit on the back of her suit smashes into a rock, a cord whipping free and snaking around like a living thing as it vents her precious oxygen.

"Cleo!" I'm sprinting after her before I can think, dropping to my knees to skid in beside her where she's sprawled on the ground.

Her lips are moving, her words trapped inside her helmet. Her eyes are huge, mouth open as if she's already struggling for air.

I grab at the cord that was venting her O_2, my gloved fingers fumbling as I yank it in close to my helmet, trying to see if the auto shutoff has worked. It's stopped wriggling, so I think it has—I can only hope there's enough air left in there to keep her going until we get inside. And we have more problems than the air, of course. Without power, the heating coils in her suit will already be cooling.

I reach for her elbow to help her to her feet, and she shakes off my hand, big brown eyes trying silently to communicate something to me. She flicks her gaze down, and when I follow it, I realize she has her right hand clapped over her left forearm in a death grip. The rocks she fell onto must have torn the suit.

Which means there's no way to know how much air she has left.

An eddy of dust swirls around us, turning her fuzzy for a moment. And that's when I realize I can't see where the garage is anymore.

The world has turned red, trapping Cleo and me in our own private dust storm, with zero visibility.

My body's turning so cold that it feels like my own suit's lost heating, but I know it's just fear. I know that—even if I can't make myself believe it. I force my breath to come more slowly, but I can hear the ragged edge to it.

Slowly, so slowly, I climb to my feet, and lean down to wrap my arms around Cleo, helping her clamber up without releasing her grip on the torn arm of her suit. She's shaking in my arms.

I walk the pair of us slowly forward, steering her toward where I think the garage entrance is. We take one step together, two, three, then ten, falling into a shuffling rhythm.

But the airlock's taking forever to show up. Am I definitely walking in the right direction?

I think so.

I have to be. It was ahead of me, a little to my right. But that was when I was moving toward it.

Which way did I end up facing when I got Cleo to her feet? Toward the garage, or away?

We're running out of time, and I don't know where we are.

Cleo's shuffling in front of me, all her concentration on keeping her suit intact. She's hyperventilating—I can feel her ribs heaving against my arms—then suddenly her legs give, and she sags in my arms, head swaying from side to side. I catch a glimpse of her face through her helmet—her lashes are fluttering, her mouth open wide, gasping for air.

Her right hand begins to peel away from her left arm, and I clamp my own hand over it, holding her ripped suit in place like a vise. That means I have to keep her moving with just one arm wrapped around her ribs.

A moment later her foot catches on another rock, and we both stumble and fall together, me desperately clinging to her. We land in a tangled heap on the ground that drives the air from my lungs, sending up more dust to join the cloud all around us. My arm lands under her and pain shoots up into my shoulder, but I force myself to keep my grip tight.

I have to hold on.

I wouldn't know which way was up if it wasn't for the ground beneath me, pressing into my sore shoulder. Red dirt's scattered across it, red dust hanging in the air as the storm moves through, every possible landmark invisible. The whole world is red.

I keep hold of the rip in Cleo's suit as she lolls onto her back. She's looking up at me in confusion, a line between her brows, and then she pushes onto her elbows, trying to get clear of me.

"Cleo, no! Stay still!" I'm shouting—when she keeps trying to wriggle free, I'm *screaming*, but she can't hear me. I'm screaming inside my own private little world, stuck inside my suit.

The realization is hitting me like a body blow, driving my own air from my lungs: *I can't lose her*.

I won't be okay without her.

I need her.

I press my helmet against hers, begging her with my eyes to understand. Starved of air, her gaze is bleary, totally bewildered. She doesn't know where she is, and I don't think she knows who I am either.

She stares up at me for a long moment, then goes obediently still.

Slowly, painfully, I start to pull the two of us to our feet. I have no idea which direction the garage is in—I have no idea where we came from in the first place.

I can't leave Cleo, because I can't trust her to keep the pressure on her suit, so I'm forced to bring her with me, walking her in front of me like a giant puppet as I stumble along in zero visibility, searching for the buildings and safety. She's almost a deadweight, more harm than help.

I walk us in each direction in turn, because I know we can't be more than twenty paces from the place where the rock and dirt gives way to the hard lines of the hab emerging from it—and if I can find that wall, I can follow it to the garage entrance.

Once I've done my twenty paces, I swivel what I desperately hope is 180 degrees, then return and try the next direction.

I do this six times, over and over, forcing myself to stay calm, ignoring the fact that now I'm hyperventilating too—my breath is coming too fast, too short, and my helmet's starting to fog up, a drop of water running down the center of my vision.

Cleo's dying in my arms, and I can't find the way to safety.

Then finally, finally, the most beautiful thing I've ever seen in my life looms up ahead of me. The edge of a straight wall, emerging from the ground like a whale breaking the surface of the ocean. It pushes up on an angle, and I stumble along it until I find the seams of the garage door.

I pin Cleo against the wall with my body to keep her upright, one hand clamped around the rip at her forearm, the other running frantically up and down the doorframe for the release.

I find the release button, pound it with my fist, and we stumble in together, the doors taking an eternity to close behind us. I feel the pressure shift, and I'm gasping inside my helmet, turning Cleo in my arms so I can check her face. Tears stream down her cheeks and her pale skin is turning gray.

It's a lifetime until the airlock equalizes. The doors to the empty garage swing open, and breathable air rushes in. I rip off my gloves and grab for the release on Cleo's helmet with a shaking hand, unlatching it and tossing it to the ground to bounce away.

She gasps a shuddering breath, lips parting, chest rising, and relief rushes through me in a trembling wave. She's still breathing. She's still here.

She's alive.

My legs fold, and together, the pair of us sink down to the floor.

21.

CLEO

2 HOURS, 55 MINUTES REMAINING

MY HEAD FEELS LIKE a watermelon somebody stomped on. Every time my heart beats, it's like another blow sends a shockwave of *ouch* through my body.

"We need painkillers," my mother says, and when I blink to focus, I find her sitting beside me.

People used to mistake her for my big sister, but over the last couple of years, age has piled onto her. I inherited my brilliantly red hair from Mom, but hers is dull now, yanked back into a messy bun to keep it out of the way. Her pale skin is shadowed underneath her eyes and there are harsh lines at the edges of her mouth.

"These are the last ones," I say, turning the silvery foil packet over in my hands. "The chem isn't going to give us any more on credit. Do you think he can last a little longer?"

She lets out a slow breath, burying her face in her hands.

She's close to breaking now, I know that. With a strange kind of sense that lives somewhere in the back of my mind, I can tell she's starting to distance herself from me. I couldn't point to anything she's done—no telling pause when she speaks, no refusal to meet my eyes. But some tiny thing that was there before—now it's gone.

Mom's going to break soon, and she's going to leave.

It's too much for her, watching Dad fade out of existence. It's too much, holding these little silver packets in our hands and knowing we'll spend the rest of our lives finding a way to pay for them.

"I can do without them," Dad said when we first got the scrips from the autodoc. When I started to argue, he reached out and took my hand in his big, warm one, giving it an easy squeeze. I looked down at the oil and grease on his knuckles, worked into the creases. Such a familiar sight.

"They're what you need," I protested.

"I know the odds, my girl. They're low. We're not taking on that kind of debt, not for—"

"So what, we should just sit here and wait for you to—" I choked on the word *die*, and he wrapped me up in his arms the way he had when I was small.

Now, don't get me wrong. As I look at her beside me, despairing over these last pills, I'm angry at my mother for what she's going to do. I'm furious. Somewhere deep inside, something's boiling, threatening to burst out of me if I let it. A special kind of rage, that she's meant to be here, she's meant to handle this, she's meant to be my *mom*, and she isn't.

But she can't help it—I know that too.

You know who *could* help it?

I turn the meds over in my fingers again, smoothing out the crinkled foil of the little packet. Tracing the shooting stars of the red-and-yellow GravesUP logo.

They could change this anytime they liked. They could make these affordable any day they wanted to. It would take one word, one decision. But they don't.

They don't even look at us. Their gaze is fixed on the stars.

"I think he needs them now," Mom whispers. "I don't think there's any point in saving them." There's a break in her voice. She cares for him, I know that. She cares for me, so much. The Mom who'll break and run soon isn't the person I've grown up with.

She's who GravesUP has made her.

I don't reply, but just tear the foil in one quick motion, shaking out the little pair of pills. It's like I'm tearing something inside myself when I do it.

The rip goes straight through the slick logo. Now, *why* does it feel like I'm supposed to remember something when I look at it?

Stomp, stomp, stomp.

My head is *killing* me.

"Cleo, open your eyes. *Please* open your eyes."

Who is that? I know that voice. It's low, husky with worry, murmuring my name like a prayer.

Hunter.

"Cleo, you have to wake up. Our ride's nearly here, you can't stop now." Someone pulls off my gloves, curling a hand around mine. The warmth of their skin feels like the sun on my eyelids when I turn my face toward it. "Please open your eyes."

Honestly, opening my eyes sounds like a terrible idea, but he sounds incredibly worried and going on a ride sounds like it could be fun. So with a huge effort, I hoist one eyelid up and take a peek, my vision swimming, the light sending tears spilling down my temples.

Then Hunter's face comes into view, gazing down at me with a ragged kind of fear that makes me reach up to cup his cheek with my hand. He is *beautiful*. Smooth brown skin, his full lower lip caught by his teeth, tousled hair falling into his eyes. He's big, broad-shouldered, but so gentle in his strength.

He grabs for my wrist and squeezes it, and makes a sound like a sob, and that's what brings the memories back.

Suddenly I hear my own sobs inside my helmet, and I remember my chest burning, and I . . . my suit. *My suit*. I twist my body, wrenching up my arm to see the gash in the fabric. It feels like a nightmare—like it happened to someone else, someone I know.

"How . . ." My voice is a rasp, and the word hurts my head.

"I don't know," he manages, running his fingers from my temple down my jawline, as though he has to touch me to be sure I'm real. "I just . . . I got you here, somehow. I thought you were going to die. I thought maybe you'd already decompressed. But I couldn't leave you there." His voice firms. "I wasn't going to leave you there."

Tears spill down my temples again, my breath releasing in a shaky exhalation.

I couldn't leave you there.

Everybody leaves me. They die, or they run, and then I'm on my own again, fending for myself.

Everybody leaves me. But Hunter . . .

Hunter stayed.

I reach up, curving one hand around the smooth skin at the back of his neck, and without a moment's hesitation, I pull his mouth down to mine. He lets out a soft breath of surprise, but he doesn't protest—in fact, it's like the bonds that have been holding him back have suddenly snapped.

He buries his hand in my hair, his lips soft on mine, his skin so warm, so alive. His thumb brushes gently against my cheek, grounding me in the here and now, his heartbeat like an anchor.

I make a faint sound, and he offers something wordless in return, my pulse quickening as I let myself take shelter in his arms. He holds me like he wants to shield me.

I lose myself in the taste of him, in this moment that's just ours, and let everything else fade away as he sets my skin on fire.

Just for a moment, the weight I carry—the weight of my past—falls away, and I let myself fly.

22.

HUNTER

2 HOURS, 53 MINUTES REMAINING

I'M LOST IN THE warmth of Cleo's skin, in the way her hand's wrapped around the back of my neck to keep me close, and I'm clinging to her just as hard. Every moment of this kiss is short-circuiting my brain, sending shivers of pleasure straight down my spine, and I—

"Hustle!" The voice is distant, and it takes me a moment to understand it came from outside the bubble the two of us have made for ourselves.

Then my head snaps up and I meet Cleo's startled gaze. That shout came from somewhere *inside* the base. The mercs are on their way.

"Shit," she whispers, shoving me away, and I scramble to climb off her and clamber to my feet. I reach down to pull her up, but her knees nearly give as she stands, and I'm forced to wrap my arms around her.

"You think they saw the outer doors open?" I whisper.

We're already moving together, and I wrap my arm around her shoulders to support her as we hobble out of the individual garage and into the main facility. It's bigger than the one on the east side, filled with maintenance benches, equipment abandoned mid-repair.

The doors hum closed behind us, the little space we just left now ready for Rover to drive in. But if she does, she'll find herself at gunpoint.

"We have to warn her," I say.

"We have to hide," Cleo replies, still clinging to me, her hair mussed from where I ran a hand through it. "Can't help her if we're dead."

I look around wildly—there are plenty of spaces to try to hide, but nowhere that'll be out of sight if they truly start searching. And if they saw that door open, they will. Then my gaze lifts and I feel Cleo shift her weight as she locks onto the same solution in the same moment. The balcony. We hid there in the east garage to spy on the mercs, and we can hide there again now.

"I can do it," she says before I can ask the question. Her ability to keep going is nothing short of staggering.

We stumble across to the balcony together, and I drop to one knee, making a stirrup out of my hands.

Without a word, Cleo steps onto it, and I push to a stand as she lifts her arms. She grips the edge of the balcony and, with a kick I have to dodge, pulls herself up. I jump to grab at the edge, with muscles that are starting to shake as the adrenaline wears off but that are still Earth-strong.

We heave ourselves up and under the railing, and flop together on the balcony like a pair of fish out of water, still gasping for breath. I don't think I can stand, but I force myself up to all fours after a minute. I crawl over to a desk, desperately hoping for a headset, and snatch one up when I find it, then crawl back to Cleo, who's wriggled around so she can look over the edge of the balcony.

I settle the headset at her temples, then lower myself down beside her, lifting one arm automatically. She shifts over to tuck herself under it. We're both still in our suits, and I wish I could feel more of her warmth against me, but she rests her temple against mine, and together we wait, caught up in this fierce twist of fear and wanting.

"Rover's going to pull in," Cleo whispers. "The best we can do is try and create a diversion, hope she realizes in time to run for it. This side of the base is closer to Ares. If they have to run back to the east side for one of their rovers, she'll have a head start."

"We could find a console, try and radio her," I murmur.

"We'd need to log in," Cleo counters. "What do you think the odds are of figuring out someone's password or faking their handprint in the next two minutes?"

"Shit," I mutter, easing away from her just enough to prop up on one elbow and look around the balcony for anything I can use as a weapon.

Cleo lets out a slow breath and speaks softly. "If we have to, we can yell for their attention. Then follow me. We can draw them off, and I can hide us." Her eyes are closed, and there's a tension in her jaw that seems like more than her reaction to the idea of having to run anywhere right now.

"Hide us where?" I ask.

"I know places they don't," she replies, but before I can press further, footsteps ring out below.

A sort of numb dizziness is churning inside me, that we came this close and our chance of escape is lost. But if we can find a way to get Rover out of here alive, then not *everything* is gone. She knows we're here. Perhaps she told someone at her base. Or perhaps they'll come looking for her.

It's exhausting to have to turn to the next round of plans, to have to find a way to pick myself back up yet again. All I want to do is rest my head on my folded arms, and close my eyes, and wish myself somewhere else.

A noise jerks my attention back to the floor below as the Pirate comes striding out, followed by the two women who hunted us in the cinema. First comes the one with the tattoo across her forehead. Then the other, small and slender, moving with an innate grace. "Ballerina," I murmur, watching her move. Dancers do well in zero g, and I bet she was one, before she got into crime.

Then the outer door of the garage opens, and a rover starts to pull in. I can imagine the woman driving it peering anxiously through the windshield for us, wondering if she got here in time, or if the invaders will spring out. She remains inside the rover for now, and for that I'm grateful.

Without a word, Cleo and I both ease up to our hands and knees, preparing our aching bodies to run.

"Station two," says the Pirate, and both of the women with him reach up to their headsets to adjust them. Beside me, Cleo does the same, and I lean in to listen. "Safe trip?" continues the Pirate, his voice coming at me both from below and through Cleo's headset. He sounds relaxed. As he should be, I guess—after all, his people are the ones holding the guns.

Eventful, says another voice through the headset, and it takes me a moment to realize it's Rover's, minus the static fuzz from the dust storm outside.

"That so?" the Pirate replies, and the back of my neck starts to prickle. Something's not right here. He sounds way too conversational.

Well, I spent the last part of it talking to a pair of civilians you've apparently got running around your base, Rover replies. *Someone want to explain what the fuck is going on?*

Ice water trickles down my spine, my body ahead of my brain as I try to understand what I'm hearing. I'm frozen in place, and I'm not sure Cleo's even breathing.

Then Ballerina speaks, hands on hips. "Are you saying there are only two of them?"

The Pirate cuts her off with a gesture. "I assure you, we've got it in—"

Do not say "in hand," Rover snaps. *They made an escape plan with me, you do not have them even remotely under control. I was hoping they'd be here to greet me, actually.*

The lighting panel outside her garage turns green, indicating the pressure inside has equalized. As we stare down at the scene below, she climbs out of the rover, her silhouette visible through the frosted panel of the door.

Bile rises in my throat and I clamp my lips together.

There is no rescue coming.

And there's maybe two and a half hours left until they blow this place up.

The door to the garage slowly rises, in time for me to see Rover bending down to pick up one of my gloves—I tore them off in my hurry to get Cleo out of her helmet and left them behind.

She turns the glove over in her hand, maybe considering how close she came to being in the same space as us. Then she comes sauntering through to the main facility, unbuttoning the neck of her suit and stretching away the cramps that come with a long drive. That's when I get my first good look at her.

I stare down at her warm brown skin. Her dark hair is pulled back into a braid. As she turns, I take in her features—keen eyes, a mouth I've seen before, lips full and always halfway to a smirk.

It's all familiar to me—I know the way she lifts her chin, the lines of her cheekbones.

We got our looks from our father.

The one behind all this is standing in clear view now.

And it's my sister, Marguerite.

23.

CLEO

2 HOURS, 45 MINUTES REMAINING

HUNTER STARTS TO CRAWL backward, away from the railing. When I glance over my shoulder at him, his golden-brown skin is pale, all the blood drained from his face.

Is this him going into shock? I think he's going to throw up.

Wordlessly I force myself up to my hands and knees so I can crawl after him. My head is pounding, my muscles aching like I've run a marathon, let them cool down, and now been stupid enough to try to stand up again. The adrenaline of the suit rupture is killing me. The no-slip metal grid on the floor hurts the palms of my hands as they press into it, but I grit my teeth and keep crawling.

The conversation coming in over my headset has gone silent—they're close enough to talk to each other now, and I'm sure the Pirate doesn't want a live broadcast of him getting his ass handed to him.

Because holy shit, the Pirate has a boss, and that boss is Rover. I can't believe how close we got to screwing ourselves by trusting her. I nearly *died* getting here.

When we make it out to the corridor, Hunter continues on through the door to someone's office, stopping just inside it and shifting to sit with his back against the wall, his arms wrapped around his knees.

Groaning under my breath, I slide the door closed behind us and settle in beside him, reaching out to rest my hand over one of his. His skin is cold for the first time, clammy.

"It's okay," I say softly. "We'll figure this out. We'll keep on surviving, and we'll do it together."

It's so wrong that I want to kiss him again right now, but for sure I do. And this change of mind isn't some unhealthy attachment because he didn't leave me behind like my shitty family did.

This is . . . I saw who he is. Who he really is. And I like who he is. I trust that guy.

I want to tell him who *I* am, and I'm going to.

Also, I want to kiss him again because I can. Because when I touch him, it's like sparks fly between us, and the heady rush of being allowed to just touch him when I want to is almost enough to drown out the *oh shit oh shit oh shit* of nearly getting caught by Rover.

Hunter tries to speak, I think, but it's as though the words get stuck in his throat. "Cleo, she . . ."

"Hunter?" I try, squeezing his hand. "What is it?"

He closes his eyes. "That's my sister," he whispers.

"What?" I ask stupidly. "Who's your sister?"

"Rover," he chokes out. "She's Marguerite. My twin sister."

I feel like I'm underwater trying to swim toward the surface, but I can't tell which way is up. "I don't understand."

"She's in charge. This is a Graves operation."

"No it's not," I begin. "It's—" But I cut myself off. What can I say? That I spoke to Sabrina behind his back, and she told me they're hacking the servers to legalize a whole bunch of hitchers?

"That's Marguerite," he insists. "She's my mother's right hand. There's no way she's here without my mother's knowledge. And that means GravesUP attacked the United Nations."

My voice is too high when I speak, strained. "Why? Why would they do that?"

"How the hell should I know?" he demands.

"They're your—"

"—family, oh, I know." His voice is low with bitterness.

I try desperately to reach for some way to make this make sense. "Well, it's better than being attacked by one of your corporate enemies, right? I'm sure they'd love nothing more than to get their hands on you."

It's as if Hunter doesn't hear me. He shakes his head, gazing at the wall opposite us. "This isn't who we are," he murmurs. "We always say we're rule-breakers, but we mean stuff like . . ."

I feel the words welling up inside me—the words I've been keeping so carefully bottled up. Every time I've bitten my tongue to avoid an argument with him over Graves is turning on me now and I can feel years of frustration and anger and fear rushing to find an outlet. "You mean stuff like breaking a

UN convention so you could blast off to Mars and settle it first? Or inviting all your friends to join you while screwing everyone you left behind on Earth?"

"We don't do that," he insists. "We play hard, but fair."

I can see him reaching for an explanation, for a reason that everything that's happened here is somehow a big misunderstanding. He's spent a lifetime dreaming about his family legacy. He'd rather twist himself in knots to justify it than face the truth.

"Hunter, please, you're smarter than this. Nothing GravesUP does is fair, you have to see that."

"I know what this looks like . . ." he murmurs.

"What this looks like is an illegal invasion of the United Nations."

"There are a lot of complex factors at play here," he mumbles, gazing at the wall opposite us. "Perhaps there's some kind of corruption—"

I hang my head. *Please*, I'm begging him silently. *Be better than this. Be who I thought you were.*

"—this isn't who we are," he repeats.

"Hunter," I snap, "GravesUP takes *everything*. Whatever they want, whenever they want it, legal or not. You're the ones who broke NASA, who abandoned 'for all mankind' and made it 'for us and our friends.'"

"It was *way* more complicated than that," he shoots back, voice low. "NASA used to be incredible. NASA used to say, 'Dare mighty things.' But they got sucked dry of all their funding, and they got small, and slow, and somebody else *had* to step up. My grandfather did."

My voice is like ice. "There is *nothing* mighty about saving yourself, and nobody else. Once you've decided you're the only ones that matter, why not take Pax? Why not kill people, to keep it all to yourself?"

"No, there's an explanation for this," he insists, ignoring my words. "We don't attack bases. We don't try to kill people."

Oh, but you do kill people! I want to scream. *I'm sorry your father died the way he did, but GravesUP kills people like my father every day. They just do it in a different way.*

They took our last penny, sent their enforcers, who then sent their bounty hunters after me even when there was nothing left. They ruined my family and then they chased me all the way to a new planet.

That's when I realize something in me has shifted. It's like I was asleep, having this lovely, stupid dream about kissing this boy. But now I'm awake, and with every word he speaks, I'm remembering who he is, what his family and their company stand for. What he would think of me, if he knew who I really was.

I swallow bitterly. I have to give up arguing about whether his family is evil and make myself focus on practicalities. I have to get back on that exhausting path toward survival that I know so well. "Well, whatever your sister and her team are doing here, do we talk to them? She isn't going to shoot you, right?"

Hunter doesn't reply.

My stomach drops. "*Hunter.* Your sister won't let them shoot you, will she?"

He just lowers his head to rest it against our joined hands.

This can't be happening. I pull my hand from his, suddenly stiff.

Either I'm going to die because his family doesn't want witnesses to what they've done here, or I'm going to die because his sister wants him dead, and I happen to be holding his hand. Just when I thought GravesUP couldn't find another way to screw me, I'm caught in the family's cross fire.

Even my last-ditch way out is blocked now. If this really is GravesUP, then Sabrina lied, or was lied to. They're obviously not here to help hitchers—this is some bigger, corporate game they're playing—and there'll be no deal for me. My chance at a new name, at a new life, at freedom—that's all gone. One by one, my ways out of this are shutting down.

My throat is thick and it feels like I can't swallow. Slowly I wrap my arms around myself, hands curling to fists.

I'm jolted from my thoughts when a voice rings out—too near for comfort, and raised in anger. "They can't have gone far."

Our heads snap up at the same time. Rover—*Marguerite*—knew we were here to meet her. Of course she's hunting for us.

Hunter looks like he's still in shock, his skin sallow, his gaze unblinking.

I knew better than to throw my lot in with someone else, and I did it anyway, and here I am. Every time I let my heart lead the way, this is what happens.

I let myself get pulled into their games, and now I'm going to die, while Hunter insists his precious corporation doesn't play like this.

Hunter moves, slowly unwinding his body, trying to get to his feet. "We have to go," he says, voice husky. "We have to hide."

"Right." I'm used to running. I can pick it up again in a heartbeat.

He might say he wants to hide with me, but Hunter's going to go down insisting that GravesUP Industries aren't the assholes I know them to be, all because he can't accept the truth about the empire his family has created. And if that's the story he's sticking with—if he insists on this level of denial—then he's not on my side. He's not on my team.

I'm on my own, like I always was.

Still, I have to stockpile every advantage I can find. Until I know if I can trade him, I'm not going to say a word.

I make myself stand, my muscles screaming a protest. I don't make eye contact. "Let's go."

Together we slip out of the office to jog along the corridor—or shuffle, really, everything hurts—taking corners quickly as I instinctively pick a route without cameras. We need another drone—looking around corners is too dangerous.

And then Sabrina's voice is in my ear, buzzing from my headset.

Cleo, we should talk. Come to the bridge. It'll just be me, unarmed. There are five exits from there—you know we don't have the people to cover them all.

My breath catches and I nearly stumble. Hunter looks back, reaching out an arm to steady me. There's concern in his eyes, a softness that makes me want to scream. Even after the argument we just had, he has no idea what I hear when he defends Graves. He has no idea anything's changed.

I make the decision in an instant, grabbing at the thought already on my mind when Sabrina dropped into my ear and twisting it into an excuse.

"We need a drone," I hear myself say. "Something that can see them before they see us. I'll grab one and meet you at the greenhouse. Keep following this corridor, you'll get there."

Hunter opens his mouth to protest, but I duck away down a hallway, turn a corner to shake him off my tail in case he's trying to follow me, and make for the bridge. I wait until I'm half a minute away from him before I reply to Sabrina.

"If you're unarmed, I want your gun where I can see it, out of your hands."

You got it, Sabrina replies.

When I reach the bridge, I stop to let my breathing slow before I walk carefully up to the entrance, every nerve on edge. I know this is stupid—I know I could be walking into danger. I know I'm letting my anger make decisions for me.

I keep moving anyway, pausing in the shadows by the doorframe, letting my gaze sweep over the space. It's empty except for Sabrina, who stands at the center, near the commander's desk.

Marguerite's team left their equipment plugged into a bunch of displays, the screens glowing brightly, but the lights around the edge of the circular room are dimmed. I don't think they were the first time I came here. I wonder why they did that.

Sabrina's clearly on alert, turning in a slow circle to scan the exits, each of which leads to a different part of the base. Her hands are held away from her sides, and her gun lies on a desk a few feet in front of her. Technically she's done what I asked—she's unarmed, and her gun's where I can see it. But it's closer to her than to me.

I wait until her back's turned, then dart forward on silent feet, hurrying to close the distance between me and the gun, my mouth dry.

I close my hand over it as she completes her circle, and she goes still when her gaze lands on me. She slowly raises her hands.

"You came," she says with a pleased smile. "Let's talk."

"I don't talk to liars," I reply, my fingers curling around the gun's grip. "You told me this job was about getting hitchers' names entered in the registers. I know who sent you now. Like hell it's about hitchers."

Sabrina inclines her head in acknowledgment. "Okay, yes," she agrees. "It's not *just* about the hitchers. And yes, it's a GravesUP operation. I admit I left that out. But I wasn't lying about the registers. I've got friends here I want to take care of, and associates who'll pay, so I got them to add in some hitchers as a part of my fee. Let the corporates fight each other if they want, Cleo. It's not our business. I'm still going to get paid, and you can be legal."

"Right, they're going to just let me climb aboard, because they're my biggest fans, after all this," I reply, and she goes a little more still when I gesture with my gun hand.

"They'll do that deal to get you to stop fucking with them," she replies. "Listen, babe, I'm not on Team Graves. I'm a merc.

I'll be off to a new hustle after this, and there's room for you on it. You've done plenty here to prove you'd be worth vouching for."

I study her, wishing desperately I could read her expression. She could be telling the truth. Or perhaps all she wants is to find a way to screw me. But then again, she didn't try to ambush me when I got here.

"You and I don't have to care about what this is," she says, with half a shrug. "We can just use it. Get paid, head to the next job."

Perhaps she really does think I'm worth having on her side, especially if she's planning on that next job being here on Mars. It's not like the population is endless. Someone who can keep it together has to be worth something.

"You're right," I say slowly. "You and I don't have to care about what this is. But I'd have to be willing to work for GravesUP if I join you now, and I don't know if I can do that."

Sabrina shrugs again. "Life's not easy here for a hitcher. I'm guessing you've had enough time to work that out. Let me get you on the register, come with me to the next job, and you don't have to think about the Graves family again."

Something prickles at the back of my neck. She's trying to reel me in too quickly. Is it a trap? But maybe she just has her eye on the clock. There're only two and a half hours left on it.

Something about this doesn't feel right.

I can still hear Hunter's voice in my head, denying everything I know, ignoring everything I tried to tell him. *This isn't who we are.*

He's part of the company that ruined my life, that invaded the United freaking Nations, and with the evidence right in front of his eyes, he still can't see the truth about them.

At least Sabrina's honest about being a terrible person.

I glance back over my shoulder to gauge the distance to the nearest exit, weighing my options.

And that's when I see Hunter standing in the open doorway, staring at me.

24.

HUNTER

2 HOURS, 28 MINUTES REMAINING

MY WHOLE BODY FREEZES in place as I realize Cleo's not alone. She's standing in the middle of the bridge facing the woman with the forehead tattoo, who . . . wait, has her hands up?

Holy shit, Cleo's got her gun.

When she turns her head and sees me, she goes perfectly still.

Turn around! I silently urge her. *Don't give the merc a chance to lunge for the gun!*

Whatever I expected when I got here, it wasn't this. I tried to tell Cleo that we'd told Rover—Marguerite—that we were in the greenhouse, so we couldn't meet there. But she tore off, and afraid to shout or draw attention, I ran after her.

"This your boyfriend?" asks the woman with her hands up.

"Shut up," snaps Cleo, in a tone that would render me silent forever if she aimed it my way.

I'm not sure what to do. I don't want to distract her or

interrupt whatever play she's making. The smallest flicker of hope is springing to life inside me—maybe she's trying to get this woman to start a rover for us?

Maybe we can run.

The woman speaks again, clearly not that bothered by Cleo's tone. "We can talk about getting him on the list too, babe."

I frown. *What exactly has Cleo been discussing with this woman?* I speak before I have a chance to think. "What list?"

The mercenary—still keeping her hands raised carefully in the air—leans to one side so she can look around Cleo. Her gaze rakes up and down me, measuring something, before she speaks again. "Wait, is he a local? I assumed you were running with another hitcher, but this boy has money written all over his pretty self."

Cleo's eyes widen and her lips part like she's looking for words but can't find them.

It takes a long moment for the woman's words to sink in. *Another hitcher.*

Cleo's . . . what?

But even in my confusion, the pieces start slotting into place, each one a new blow, each one sending me reeling. It all fits together.

Cleo never told me why she didn't make it off base during the evac. I was too busy to ask that first time I found her on the bridge.

But if she wasn't supposed to be here, that explains why she didn't want to pick anything up from her quarters when I offered. She doesn't *have* quarters.

It explains how she knew so many back ways and shortcuts.

She told me just a couple of minutes ago in the garage that she knows places others don't. She told me we couldn't radio Rover to warn her because we didn't have a password to log into a console. I didn't even think to ask about *her* password.

Cleo lied her way onto Mars, then she pretended to listen, to *care* as I showed her the pieces of my heart. And all along she was lying to me at every turn about who she was. A hitcher. One of the people who stole my father from me. Did she think they were justified? Did she agree with them?

"No," I say slowly, trying to push through the numbness, to find some kind of feeling on the other side. "I'm not another hitcher. I take it you two know each other?"

"Aw," says the woman, lowering her hands and planting them on her hips. "Cleo, you didn't tell him about us? Kid, the two of us go way back. We've been talking about options for an exit strategy for a while now. Not a great time to be at Pax. I was just explaining to Cleo that she doesn't actually need to die today. And by *today*, I mean in two and a half hours, actually, so we should keep this moving."

"Shut up, Sabrina," Cleo says softly.

"How do you know her?" I ask, though I know the answer.

Cleo won't meet my gaze—she's still gripping the gun, but it's pointed at the floor, and she's staring at a drink bottle someone left behind on their desk like it holds all the answers she knows she owes me.

What does *talking for a while* mean?

The lights flicker overhead, and Cleo lifts her gaze briefly, eyes narrowing as she studies the fittings.

"For a moment," I say quietly, "I actually thought I knew you."

Cleo flinches, her mouth tightening, but she doesn't reply. What could she say?

"I thought I knew you," I say again, softer still. "I guess I was wrong."

This is why you don't give a piece of yourself to anybody. All you're doing is making yourself vulnerable. And when you do, they hurt you.

One way or another, they leave.

And sometimes it turns out they were never there at all.

25.

CLEO

2 HOURS, 23 MINUTES REMAINING

SABRINA'S LIPS CURVE INTO a slow smile and she cocks her head at me. "Cleo, am I in the middle of a lover's tiff right now?" she asks, far too pleased with herself. "And I thought we had something special, babe."

"Stop it," I snap. I have to think quickly—I have to pick a side. The guy who won't stop defending Graves, or the woman who's working for them? Am *I* willing to work for them?

Maybe, if it'll save my life. I've done a lot of things to stay alive. I ran all the way to another planet to stay alive.

My brain's mapping the options at lightning speed, as my grip on the gun tightens.

Sabrina: Willing to work with me, has an idea for getting me out of this, but can't guarantee she'll be able to sell me as a new recruit. If it works, though, I know what that future looks like. I've lived it before.

Hunter: Looking at me like he'd rather die than side with me, but he's a Graves—powerful enough to protect anyone, if he wants to. *If* he wants to.

Then a new voice sounds. "Is it finally time for introductions? I've been looking forward to this."

The Pirate comes striding into the room, gun raised. He's even bigger than he looked from the balcony, a broad-shouldered bruiser. He's not handsome, but there's something about him that makes you look at him.

Another of the mercs—the one Hunter called the Ballerina—is just a step behind him, wearing a mean expression.

I snap my own gun up to point it at Sabrina's head, and her hands fly into the air again as she takes a step back.

"Easy now," says the Pirate in a low voice, training his gun on me. "Let's talk. And you, stay still."

For a moment I think the words are meant for me, and then I realize Hunter's eased two steps back toward the door, hoping to vanish into thin air while we all point guns at each other. He stops where he is, expression stony.

"You really are kids," the Pirate says slowly. "I didn't believe it."

The words *I'm seventeen, actually* almost make it out, but nothing makes you sound younger than protesting your age. So I fall back on what worked last time: sass. "Embarrassing, right? You with all the guns, and you're still running around after us?"

"I told you, Nico," Sabrina chimes in. "Amateurs can be more dangerous than professionals."

Did she let his name slip by accident, or is she trying to give me something as a show of good faith?

Nico shakes his head, allowing himself a hint of a smile. "Not our finest hour," he agrees. "But it's over now. We can all do math. Two guns on one. Three people on two. I admire what you've managed, truly I do, but this is when it stops. You still have a chance to choose how that happens."

Sabrina lowers her voice, the edge gone now, as she pitches her words for me alone. "Come on, Cleo. Be smart. I don't actually want to dispose of your corpse."

Above us the lights flicker again, and when they settle, the room's a touch dimmer. It's as if the power reduced a fraction, but none of the things Hunter and I did around the station should have caused that. I'm guessing from the quick frown that just crossed Nico's face that they're not taking credit either.

So what could be . . . ? *Oh.*

And just like that, I see the path forward. It's like someone's switched on floodlights and the way ahead is clear. I know exactly how to walk it.

"I'm not surrendering to you," I say, shifting my grip on my gun. Then, just as Nico starts to sigh, I continue. "But I'll join you. And I can keep the station powered up for a few hours more."

Nico takes a step closer. "You can undo this?" he asks, and whether he means it to or not, a hint of urgency makes it past his shields.

"We didn't create your power-drainage problem," I say. "This is the solar failing. It's why the cafeteria was dimmed before, why the lights wouldn't turn on in the movie theater. The station is shutting everything down in order of priority. The dust storm's coating the panels."

I see the moment he doesn't believe me—his brows lift, a quick huff of breath escaping. "It's only been a few hours," he replies. "The batteries will hold longer than that."

"Sure, under the right circumstances." I can't believe I didn't see this earlier. "Let me guess: You timed all this for the dust storm, so you could avoid satellites getting a look at you. Smart, except the same dust that protected you is blocking all the sun. The solar arrays here just aren't as good as at Graves—the UN's broke. Everything here is donated or bargain basement. If there were engineers here, they'd be switching over to backup batteries, reducing usage to get through the dust storm. But they all ran away on the evac shuttles, and nobody's here to follow the protocols."

There's a long pause as he sorts through that, looking for the holes in my argument. Then he tips his head back to study the lights. "Well, fuck," he mutters.

"I can fix it," I say with more confidence than I feel. "For a ride out of here. I've spent three months climbing around in the guts of this station and I'm good with hardware. I can reduce your usage enough to get you through a little longer."

Nico glances at Hunter. "And him?"

I snort, and ignore the feeling of Hunter's gaze boring into the side of my head. Whatever doubts he has about his sister, there's not a chance in hell that Graves staff are going to hurt him. Not when his mama's waiting for him at their compound. "I don't think he's in any danger," I say. "Bring him back to your boss, see what she thinks. Turns out they're acquainted."

That's enough to pique Nico's curiosity, and his eyes narrow as he considers the pair of us. But the Graves twins don't have public images. Nico doesn't know who Hunter is.

They walk us to the engineering department without restraints, but definitely at gunpoint. Hunter's by my side, but gazing straight ahead, his handsome jaw clenched so hard it looks like he's going to crack a tooth.

"What would you have done if I'd told you who I was when we met?" I say softly, glancing sideways and up at him. "Would you have teamed up with a hitcher?"

A flicker of his expression admits the truth we both know. *Never.* "There have been other moments since then," he says quietly, gaze still straight in front of us. "You could have—"

"Let's keep conversation to a minimum," Nico calls from behind us, and we fall silent.

He's going to be fine, I remind myself. In a few minutes he'll be back with his family, and by tonight he'll probably be soaking in a fancy bubble bath or something, thinking dark thoughts about evil hitchers.

The main engineering offices are situated near the eastern garages, where my new friends arrived at the station. Downstairs and deeper underground is the workshop where we wrapped the Boxer in expanding foam, and on this upper level is a large room full of workstations.

Across the hall is the chief's office, where we hid under a desk and I nearly let Hunter Graves kiss me.

"You sit there, handsome," Sabrina tells him, gesturing to a workstation. I see the way his gaze runs over the setup as he folds himself into a chair—he's wondering if he can log in.

He left his cuff in the greenhouse, though—he's just an onlooker now.

The Ballerina walks ahead of us and takes her place at a station that looks like a patient in the ICU, covered with stick-on patches and wires—I'm guessing this is how they hacked into it. Nico rests a hand on my shoulder and steers me over to join her.

"Grace is going to take you through the station's systems," he says. "You're going to figure out what can be turned off to save power, what can be reduced, and what you can redirect."

"And the first thing you're going to do," Grace the Ballerina adds, with a glare as cold as the Martian air outside, "is show me where to shut down power to the damn classroom, so we can get my girlfriend off a desk."

"Yeah, of course," I mutter. "You would have had trouble finding it—this place was built in stages, expanded every time they got more funding, so some of the connections aren't where you think. I can show you if you get a diagram up. We'll have to do it manually, though."

"We have to go on-site?" She narrows her gaze, trying to figure out whether I'm just looking for a chance to get away. "The boss has an all-access pass to the systems with that cuff she wears."

"And some of it's not attached to the systems," I reply. "It just got put together when they got the budget. It's not hard. You can get to the wires no problem, and they're easy to pull out. They were thinking about maintenance, not sabotage, when they built it. Just have to watch for the live ones."

"Girl, *you'll* be watching for the live ones," Grace mutters.

Nico huffs a soft laugh behind me, and I can still feel Hunter's gaze boring into a spot between my shoulder blades, though whether he's madder that I'm undoing our hard work, or that I'm a filthy hitcher, I don't know.

I have to remind myself that I don't care what the corporates do to each other. I care about what I need, and about keeping my own ass intact. This is the only way to do that, and I can't believe I nearly forgot that. I knew better than to rely on anyone but myself.

If this is what it takes, I'll hold my nose and do business with them. And if Sabrina does somehow get me out of here, I'll do what I can with that chance.

I look down at the tattoos curling their way up my forearms—at the purple flowers and green vines, a reminder that there's *always* a way, even if it's through a crack in the concrete. I'll find my way now. I'll make it.

Then I hear Nico speak again, somewhere behind me. "Now, my boy. Indulge me as I give you a pat-down, and then we'll go talk to the boss."

Hunter is about to meet his sister. I wish I could—

"Here," says Grace, pulling up a schematic. "Show me exactly where to find the power shutoff."

So, wishing I felt better about the choice I've made, and desperately trying to ignore the queasy feeling in my stomach, I do.

26.

HUNTER

2 HOURS, 11 MINUTES REMAINING

MY SISTER HAS HER feet up on the chief engineer's desk. I have a moment to study her as Nico shoves me through the door.

Her thick curls are pulled back into their usual braid, and for the first time in our lives, her skin is a little paler than mine—she hasn't been outdoors without a pressure suit in over a year. Atmosphere aside, Martian radiation is no joke. She's leaner too, maybe down a little muscle in the lighter Martian gravity.

She's wearing the same slim cuff on one wrist as I was until I left the greenhouse, but hers gleams, and the display it's projecting into the air is bright, buzzing with numbers. This must be a new Graves prototype—it looks similar to mine, but based on the specs I can see dancing in the air, this is definitely my cuff's big sister.

I'll bet its system access is much slicker too. I want it because

I want it—because it's the kind of tech I was raised to play with—but I also want it because whoever has that thing owns Pax Station, I'm sure of it.

"Mmm?" She doesn't look up from her work, levering her feet against the edge of the desk to tip the chair onto its two back legs.

Nico pauses behind me, one hand on my shoulder, probably realizing in this moment that he doesn't actually know why he brought me in, except that Cleo told him he should. "This one . . ."

He trails off, and that makes Marguerite look up, her brow creasing in the start of a question. And then her gaze lands on me.

I've never seen my sister shocked like this, not in all our eighteen years. She nearly tips the chair over backward, then scrambles to recover, surging to her feet as it thumps into place. Her cuff's display flares wildly, then goes dark.

"What are you—?" But her words die out as suspicion kicks in, her green eyes turning wary.

"I checked him for weapons," says Nico, who still has no idea what's going on.

"And scars?" she snaps.

"What?"

"She wants to know if I've been surgically altered to look like her twin brother," I supply. This is how they taught us to think, growing up. For a moment, I even consider going that route—but though I don't know what my reception's going to be as Hunter Graves, I'm pretty sure it'd be worse as an impostor.

"What?" Nico manages, but both Marguerite and I are ignoring him now.

I sigh. "In the middle of the night before our fifth birthday, we got out of bed and snuck down to the kitchen and ate our birthday cake."

Her lips part and then she shakes her head—and she's right. Someone could have gotten that out of one of the staff. Or our dad could have told someone—he thought it was hilarious. Mom didn't.

"And I told you we had to finish it, because if you leave out an unfinished meal, it attracts ghosts," I continue. "So we both kept eating until we nearly threw up." That part only the two of us could know. Marguerite stares at me, and I give her some jazz hands. "Surprise?"

"You're meant to be on Earth," she whispers. For my sister to say something as bleedingly obvious as that, she must be *rattled*. "Nico," she snaps. "Out."

"Marguerite," he says, his tone a warning all by itself.

"Out," she says again, not taking her eyes off me. A moment later, I hear the door close behind him. Damn, that guy moves silently.

"I know I'm meant to be on Earth," I say. "I wanted . . ." But I fall silent instead of finishing my sentence. I wanted to force a confrontation. To elbow her aside and slot myself into her place as Mom's heir. Power, in my own right. I sure didn't come to play happy families. I'm a Graves, after all.

Marguerite has spent five years and more cementing herself

as Mom's sidekick. If she ends me now, her competition will be gone and nobody will ever have to know.

But something strange is happening. Her expression starts to soften, the crease between her brows smoothing away, one hand coming up to hold the end of her braid, like she did when we were kids. "I can't believe it's you," she whispers.

And then my sister practically vaults the desk, throwing herself at me, wrapping her arms around me, burying her face in my shoulder. Bewildered, I lift my arms and wrap them around her carefully in return.

I dreamed of this for years—of being together, of being two halves of the same whole. And now she's here again. She's real.

"You should have told me you were coming," she mumbles into my filthy shirt. "I could have helped." Keeping hold of my shoulders, she draws back to look me in the eye. "But . . . you didn't trust me?"

Of course not! Mom abandoned me and you never once reached out, so clearly the situation suited you fine. You made yourself her only child and now you're ready to steal my half of our inheritance. But this isn't the moment for truth. I don't want to risk a lie, though—that's dangerous, around someone who knows me so well. "It was hard to know what to think," is where I settle.

"Please." She snorts. "Hunter, I never left you. *They're* the ones who separated us. And I told her that with Dad gone, you were alone. I told her you had to come here."

My brain's slowly folding in on itself and I don't know how to make words right now. She's *pleased to see me*?

Marguerite squeezes my shoulders, drinks in my face. "You didn't think you'd be welcome," she says softly.

"No, I asked," I say quietly. "I asked Mom to let me come here, over and over, even before Dad died. She said no."

"Because she's good at business, but she's terrible at family," Marguerite whispers. "I hate that you were alone back on Earth. Hunter, it was *never* me who shut you out." She's fierce as she speaks. "That was all Mom."

"Why did she do it?" I hate how pitiful that question sounds. But I *know* I was as capable as Marguerite when we were young. I've never understood why my mother would just discard me, and now, faced with the chance to ask . . .

"I think you reminded her of Dad," Marguerite says, still gazing at me, as though she's looking for that resemblance. "Hunter, I begged her to let me see you. For years. I know what she is as well as you do. But if we work together, Graves can be ours. There's room for both of us in this. You're my brother."

"Marguerite, I—" My heart strains and contracts almost painfully, my tiredness washing over me in a wave. I'm so tired. I don't know what to believe. "That time in London, I was miserable without you, and you . . ."

A shadow crosses her face, like clouds across the sun. "Wait," she says slowly, her grip on my shoulders tightening. "Wait, Hunter. No. You thought it was *me*? That I was cutting you off?" Her eyes widen in visible shock. "That one time we talked, *you* hung up on *me*!"

"You were partying in a hotel suite!" The words burst out of me.

"What, I was supposed to be dead?" she snaps. "I was trying to be normal. I was trying to show Mom I was fine, so she'd give me more freedom, so I could get to you." She shakes her head slowly. "Hunter, you're my *brother*. And I was a kid when she yanked me away. It wasn't like Dad was willing to let go of you. I would never have left you if I wasn't forced. *Never*."

And now that memory of her in the hotel suite, eyes bright with laughter as she answered the vid call, is dimming alongside the memory of the way they had to peel her off me when they separated us. The way she jumped over the desk just now the moment she knew it was me.

It's like there are two versions of Marguerite standing in front of me, side by side. There's the girl I grew up with, and the ruthless creature she became. Or that I *thought* she became.

But the more she talks, the more that certainty fades away. The easier it is to see the girl who was once my other half.

My brain tells me to go for it—that Marguerite's standing here, offering me everything I wanted.

My heart's fighting itself. It tried to love Mom, and she never loved me back. It did love Dad, and then one day he was gone. And outside is Cleo—it tried to trust her, and she lied about who she was.

But Marguerite, maybe . . . Part of my bruised heart desperately wants to trust my sister.

I lift my hands to rest them on her shoulders in return. "Mom's going to be furious," I whisper.

Marguerite's smile is conspiratorial. "We can handle her.

After what we're going to do for GravesUP here, she'll let us write blank checks."

A faint strand of relief starts to wind its way through me. Maybe I *can* have both. Someone who has my back, *and* the chance to step up at last. To do something worthy of my grandfather's legacy. There must be a reason she's here that makes sense. This is my sister, after all.

She sees the moment of decision on my face and nods. "I'm glad nobody shot you," she says.

The reminder brings me back to the present moment with a jolt.

"Yeah . . . can we start with what you're doing invading the UN?" I ask. "I heard your people talk about upping the oxygen levels and blowing this place up in, what, about two hours?"

"That's on the to-do list," she admits, finally letting go of me and circling around behind the desk once more to sink into her chair. I take the visitor's chair on the opposite side, and at exactly the same time, we rock our chairs back to rest our boots against the edge of the desk. Some stuff is just genetics, I guess.

"This is the UN," I point out. "I mean, at risk of stating the obvious."

"That's why we're here," she agrees. "Have you been in the system?"

"Sure. I saw your people going through the registers."

"Huh." She's thoughtful. "They should have seen *you*. Did you see what we're spoofing? Orbital thinks this place has completely vented and is repressurizing now."

There's a glee to her tone that worries me, and I'm trying

and failing to think of any scenario in which, based on what she's just said, GravesUP aren't the bad guys. But the fact that I haven't thought of it doesn't mean it's not there somewhere.

"It's a great way to empty a place out, an evacuation," she says. "Speaking of which, why weren't you evacuated?"

"I wasn't registered yet," I say. "Nobody knew to save me a seat."

Marguerite studies me for a moment, shaking her head. "That's spectacularly bad luck," she replies. "Then again, spectacularly *good* luck I'm the one who showed, so I guess it's a wash. Anyway, we needed the false signal to give us some time to ourselves. You know every Martian settlement is registered here, yes? Neutral third party."

"Sure."

She grins. "They also register their remote access codes with Pax. The UN acts as a central trustee, so that in an emergency, say if the staff at a settlement were incapacitated by illness or an environmental event, someone can remotely control what's happening from here."

I shake my head slowly. "Getting into those would take a lot of time, even for us. They'd have them locked down tighter than Mom's wallet."

"Not if everybody ran out of here without shutting down properly," Marguerite replies.

Something's shifting inside me, my stomach turning over as my uneasiness grows. I keep my voice even, but I sound off to my own ears, my mouth going dry. "Okay, clever. What are you going to do with the access codes?"

"I'm going to blow a bunch of basic systems, so whole settlements empty out. Six of them, to be exact."

"Six different bases?"

"Right. Keep up, Hunter. Here at Pax, we could do it by hacking in and setting off the alarms, but that won't work for the settlements we're targeting—smaller ones, mostly. They don't have great software, so we'll have to actually blow the seals."

"You're going to—" I cut myself off, my gut tightening in appalled anticipation. "Okay, then what?"

"Legally, that'll mean they've been abandoned, and all we have to do is roll in some GravesUP Industries troops, and we can take possession."

"By *abandoned*, do you mean everyone will be dead?"

Her mouth twists with regret. "Yes."

My heart's beating too fast, as if my body's getting ready to run, or fight, but I force my thoughts to slow, so I can absorb what my sister's saying.

"Okay," I say slowly. "And we're doing this because the current tenants are . . . ?"

"Wasting what they've got," she replies. "These are resource-rich areas, and we can extract a lot more value from them than these little operations. We're looking at close-to-surface mining operations, and significant ice reserves." She raises her hands to indicate her own helplessness. "This is the argument we've been having about Mars since before Grandpa Michael's time. Resources are scarce. Sites like that have to go to the ones who can make the most of them. If GravesUP is going to keep expanding, we need more to work with."

"And Mom knows you're doing this?" I ask, trying to keep the rasp out of my voice, dread curling through me now.

"Of course," Marguerite replies. "Hunter, I'm not a monster. This has all been debated, debated *again*, looked at from all angles. It's not a step to take lightly."

"Not going to make a lot of difference to the ones who get—Marguerite, you're talking about killing people. A lot of people."

"Not as many as it could be," she counters. "We're targeting smaller places, like I said. Nobody who would have the legal resources to fight us. Smaller corporations, some international alliances."

"And you'll have Graves folks march in, roll the bodies to one side, and take over," I say slowly, trying to rally myself.

I thought I'd do anything to grab my mother's attention. And I've done plenty—I've elbowed aside execs, I've fought for companies and takeovers in court. But this . . . ?

My sister's lost her mind.

And I have to be incredibly careful about what I do next, or I'll lose more than that. "You don't think people will think it was us, what with the Graves teams all ready to jump in and occupy these settlements?"

"If they do think so, they won't be able to prove it," she replies. "We'll make it look like our teams scrambled when it happened, on rescue missions for survivors. All of them have been provided with legitimate reasons for being near the targeted bases. Unfortunately they won't find any survivors, and then, well—we'll claim what's left behind, legally. Pax itself is going to blow at exactly the same time as the other six bases. That'll take out any evidence we were here, or that Pax was hacked. We'll argue that when Pax blew, a systems malfunction must have caused the other bases to go up."

"Clever," I make myself say, trying to keep my tone normal.

She sighs. "The scale GravesUP operates on—the scale we *have* to operate on—can't afford to take individuals into account. Not unless they're key personnel, like us. We have to be selective about who gets what, based on what they can *do* with it."

My mouth is completely dry now, her words replaying in my head. How many times have I said some version of this to myself? That we have to focus on who can make the most of this place.

Did I sound like my sister when I said it? Like a murderer?

"I know," I manage, quietly amazed at how normal my voice sounds. "If we want to make Mars viable for all, we have to expand."

"For all?" Marguerite shrugs. "Let's focus on making it viable for us, right now. First on the hit list is the West African Union."

I rub my hand across my mouth as my stomach flips over, trying to push down the sensation that I might throw up. "Man. They came all the way to another planet just to get screwed again."

"Mmm, sucks," she agrees. "But you know what we say. Rule-breaking has always been our thing."

It feels like I'm stepping outside my body, watching myself struggle to stay neutral. *Blank face*, I coach myself. *Keep breathing. Don't give her anything. Your life depends on it. And so do a lot of others'.*

"What about your crew?" I ask. "There are seven of them here. They'll all keep quiet on what happened?"

"Don't worry about them," she says firmly. "So? You in?"

"You're about to be a busy girl," I say. "I can see why you could use an ally. I've got your back."

"Feels good," she replies. "You hungry?"

Before me, one version of Marguerite flickers and disappears. This isn't the girl I played with as a kid. Maybe that girl never existed at all. This Marguerite is the one who installed herself as our mother's right hand.

Is her relief at seeing me now genuine, or an act? I honestly don't know. She's clearly capable of deceiving herself.

What I do know is that she's as cold and hard as our mother—maybe worse. And though I thought I wanted to be like our mother too, I'm realizing now that I never understood what that meant.

I'm utterly alone here, and I'm all that stands between my sister and six bases full of innocent people.

I told Cleo that this isn't who we are. I knew we were ruthless, but I never thought we were supervillains. In this moment, I'm realizing I was as wrong as I could have been.

If I want to be able to say that—to tell her, to tell *anyone* that GravesUP Industries fights hard, but fair—then it's up to me to prove that this isn't who we are. It's up to me to stop this.

The question is, how the hell am I supposed to do that in two hours?

"You know," I say, "I am hungry, actually. What's the chance of a snack around here?" I unfold from my chair, rising to my feet and stretching slowly. She watches me without a hint of concern.

"Maybe scare up a change of clothes, too," she suggests. "But don't be long. We're on the clock."

27.

CLEO

2 HOURS REMAINING

HUNTER COMES WALKING OUT of the chief engineer's office, side by side with his sister, and now I can see how similar they are. He's a little taller, her face is a little harder, but you can tell the same factory spat out the pair of them.

I'm sitting with Sabrina and Grace at a desk that used to belong to a guy who tacked up pictures of every dog he ever met, and the divide between Hunter and me couldn't be more obvious.

He's a Graves, standing there with the boss. I'm a nobody, sitting here as a prisoner of her employees. Sabrina keeps trying to talk to me—I think she's trying to humanize me in front of Grace—but I can't make myself respond beyond a mumble.

What did he and his sister talk about in there?

The gap between Hunter and me isn't the only reason I'm wondering about my life choices, though. The vibe in here doesn't feel good—there's a tension I don't like singing through the air. And I still don't know what they're here for. I only know it's more than altering a few registers.

Sabrina nudges me, and I snap out of it. "Let's go," she murmurs, drawing my attention back to my work.

"On it," I mutter, squinting again at the schematics Grace is pulling up. "There's a switchboard there," I tell her, pointing at the place on the display. "It doesn't show on the plans, but a whole bunch of other things are wired in there that shouldn't be." I used it for that exact reason—so many extra departments had wired in power sources that my usage would never stand out. I remember silently thanking my father as I did it—I'll never be as good as he was, but he taught me enough to make my own mods. "If you cut the power at that switchboard, you'll save more than it looks like."

Hunter's talking to his sister, and Nico hands him a meal pack from the team's stash—after the way we drugged the Martian, they're sticking strictly to their own rations, I guess. Nico's scowling behind his eye patch, probably wondering how he went from trying to kill Hunter to serving him lunch. Probably wondering if Hunter's the vengeful type.

Speaking of vengeful, I've eavesdropped enough to figure out where most of the Graves team are, right now.

The Martian's still sleeping it off. Mr. Chin-Up has been released from the freezer, and he's pissed off but fine. Currently, he's chipping the expanding foam off the Boxer, presumably stopping to pick up ball bearings at regular intervals. And Blue Braid will be back on duty once we cut the power to her section.

"What about the greenhouse?" Grace says beside me. She's finely built, and walks like she weighs nothing at all, every movement elegant and efficient.

"Shut it down, you mean?" I sit back in my chair, wrapping one arm around my middle. "That place is full of plants, though, they won't survive the cold. There're fish too, zillions of them."

Grace blinks at me. "You do understand that it's not going to be there when we leave anyway, right?"

On my other side, Sabrina nudges me again, and I make myself nod. "Yeah, of course. I'll have to go and disconnect it on-site, though. They didn't want anyone shutting it down by accident, so it's like life-support equipment—you have to do it in person. I can literally just rip the cables out."

Hunter is suddenly standing above us. My head snaps up—I didn't know he was listening. "If you're heading to the greenhouse, I'll come too," he says, as conversational as if we're talking about just going out for a walk on a nice day.

"We're a little short on time," his sister says from behind him, arms folded.

"I won't be long," he promises. "I brought one of Dad's sculptures with me, and my bag's there. I don't want to leave it behind."

She softens, inclining her head. "Sure, you grab it."

Then Nico's by her side, looking like he invented the word *looming*. "I'll handle escort," he says.

"My brother doesn't need an escort," Marguerite replies crisply. If there's some sort of Nico vs. Hunter thing going on here, Nico needs to watch himself, because his boss has chosen a side.

"Sure," Nico soothes. "I just want to see the greenhouse." He and Marguerite share a look, and I don't miss the moment he flicks his gaze at me. He might not be willing to fight her on Hunter, but it's not hard to convince her I need watching.

And so we head to the greenhouse. I'm in front, and Hunter falls easily into step with me. Nico follows us, in quiet conversation with Grace, both of them with their hands on their weapons as soon as we're out of Marguerite's sight.

I thought it couldn't get quieter around here, but now that the fans are gone—shut down as part of our energy-saving efforts—we're in a sort of muffled silence that feels like exactly what it is: the station dying.

I glance sidelong at Hunter. Now that he has his back to Nico and Grace, he looks incredibly strained—not at all like a guy who just found out he's still in charge of this situation. His hair's unkempt, as though he's been dragging his fingers through it, curls all out of place. His lips are pressed into a thin line, muscles tense.

Part of me still can't forget he's a Graves—can't believe I ever did.

But another part still wants to believe he's the boy I've been through this with. The boy who held his breath and waited for permission to kiss me. Who didn't leave me behind out there in the dust storm, but fought for my life like it was his own. Who held me like I was all that was keeping him afloat. Part of me still wants to reach out to him.

Except he's refusing to make eye contact with me, staring straight ahead as we walk, jaw squared.

Do I want to say something to him because he's the closest connection I have to the top of the tree right now? Is it my instinct for safety that drives that urge? Or is it because he's Hunter?

"So," I say softly, testing the waters.

His gaze slides sideways, though he doesn't break his stride. For a moment, our eyes lock, before his gaze flicks ahead once more. He doesn't reply, but he's listening.

"Remember at the start of all this, when we were on the bridge, we joked that we could claim this place? And you said we couldn't, because technically I was staff, so the base wasn't abandoned?" I manage a feeble smile. "Guess you could have saved yourself a lot of trouble, planted the GravesUP flag right then and there."

He closes his eyes for a moment, jaw clenched, but his expression doesn't even flicker. He gives me nothing else. It's like I took a jab at him, rather than trying for a weak joke.

My throat thickens, and for a moment there's a dangerous ache behind my eyes. I swallow hard.

This is the reminder I need. Whatever my stupid heart wants to believe, Hunter's not on my team. I have to watch my own back.

I've given him too much already—parts of myself I swore I'd keep safe from now on. I have to remember that I don't belong in his life.

1 HOUR, 53 MINUTES REMAINING

The warm air of the greenhouse washes around me as we walk through the door, and it nearly brings tears to my eyes. Coming back here feels like stepping into a haven I'd lost. Plants trail down from their frames and burst from their pots, and the rich scent of damp dirt fills my nostrils. Fish glide silently, serenely around their pond. Something inside me releases, a little more at peace—the animal part of me wants to be around nature and knows that for a moment, it is.

It feels like a lifetime ago that Hunter and I were here, eating tomatoes and a stolen pack of cookies, planning wild schemes that we so nearly pulled off. Everything's changed since then.

I walk over to the main control panels against the wall, hunting through the tools set down nearby until I find a crowbar. Digging it into one of the seams around the edge of the panel, I start wrenching the cover off.

Hunter makes his way over to the plants where he stashed his bag. I watch him sidelong as he pulls his cuff from the bag's side pocket and discreetly slips it onto his wrist.

Nico and Grace part ways and start to explore. Each of them keeps me in sight, but a greenhouse is a treat nobody wants to miss on Mars.

I pull the cover free and set it aside, then crouch to look at the spaghetti tangle of wires I've revealed. I hate that I'm doing this—the idea of killing a place like this makes me ache—but if it's the plants or me, I'm going to choose me.

Off to my right, Hunter stretches like a guy trying to be super casual, then comes sauntering over to join me in looking at the wires. He lifts one hand to cover his mouth and angles his body away from Nico before he talks.

Hunter is not good at stealth.

"We need to talk," he murmurs.

"Now you want to talk?" I mutter, eyes on my work.

"Cleo, please," he whispers. "I have a thousand apologies to make, let me start with one. We don't have much time."

I don't say anything for a moment, yanking a wire free of its connector as I start to shut down the heating system.

My head and my heart are right back into the same battle they've been waging since his sister arrived. Since before that. I don't want to talk to Hunter Graves. And also, I do, because my heart still doesn't know who this boy is.

"Just a minute," I mutter, and yank out another wire. Then I rise to my feet, turning so my back's to Hunter.

"You done?" Nico calls from across the room.

"Not even close," I call back. "But I can't shut everything down at once, or a fail-safe kicks in. This is the greenhouse, it's protected. Something goes wrong, you know how hard it is to convince the neighbors to hook you up with more seeds, fresh fish? I've done a few, now I need to wait a few minutes before I keep going." I mean, who knows? That could be true. Sounds good.

Nico's silent a long moment, but he doesn't know if I'm telling the truth, and I did yank some wires out, after all.

I let out a slow breath and drop my voice until it's almost inaudible. There's only one way to do this, and I know it. "Get in close," I murmur. "Touch me."

"What?" Hunter's reply is soft but startled.

I roll my eyes. "You're a Graves. Nico sees you getting up close and personal, he's going to give us a minute. You want privacy, this is how we get it." Nico may not trust Hunter, but he'll still want to be on his good side. Man's smart.

There's a long pause from behind me. "I'm sorry about this," Hunter says softly. And then he does as I told him to do, stepping into my space, curving an arm around my waist.

Shock runs through me as my body catches fire. I lean back into him as a shiver runs up my spine, tilting my head to one side to offer up my neck. When he drops his head to brush his lips against the bared skin, electrical currents zip through me to my fingertips. This reaction was *not* part of the plan.

But this is what I could have had. How is the guy who makes me feel like *this* also a Graves? The universe still manages to be unfair in ways I never imagined, despite all the times it's screwed me already.

Trying to mask the strength of my response, I turn in his arms, curl a hand around his shirt and tug on it. He walks me back until I bump up against a desk, arm still around my waist, hand resting in the curve of my spine. A curtain of vines partially conceals us now—but Nico can still see two pairs of legs, and the outline of our bodies, so he doesn't object.

"I was wrong," Hunter whispers, keeping in close. He sets my skin tingling again, but I force myself to pay attention.

"Yes," I agree. "Please provide a comprehensive list of ways in which you were wrong."

He doesn't even give me a flicker of a smile. His lips press together, brows drawing down, and he closes his eyes a moment, exhaling softly before he speaks. When he does, though, he meets my eyes. "Cleo, this *is* who we are. We don't fight fair. We break rules, and we kill people."

His words take me utterly by surprise. It's as though they break down a dam inside me, my pulse kicking up a level, as heat of a different sort rushes through me. I've been screaming into the void for so long that GravesUP is evil—the shock of hearing it from Hunter unleashes something.

Words surge up in me, but I stay close to him, his arms around me, as they pour out in a furious whisper. "Damn right it's who you are. It always was. It was GravesUP that charged my father more than his yearly salary for his meds. It was Graves that sold the debt to the gangs that sent me running. I didn't run all the way to Mars because I wanted to; I ran because it was my only choice."

Hunter jerks back from me, and by instinct I keep hold of his arms to stop him from breaking away and alerting Nico. Hunter closes his eyes, and I see the sorrow written on his face, in the twist of his mouth, the way the lines of his jaw go hard. "And we got you anyway, however far you ran," he whispers.

I feel tears burning behind my eyes. "You did."

Hunter swallows, forcing himself to meet my gaze. "My whole life, I didn't see," he whispers. "All of it has been a lie.

I thought the fact that we created things nobody else could, that we did things nobody else could, gave us the right—the duty, even—to keep going."

I reach up to touch my fingertips to his cheek. "More than one thing can be true," I murmur. "What your grandfather did, getting to Mars? That was extraordinary. Doing it to build a lifeboat for himself, instead of a place that could save so many others? Not worth it."

"Never worth it," he whispers. "I understand why you didn't tell me who you were. I'm so sorry you had to lie."

I trail my fingers down his jawline, trying not to let him see the way something inside me is unclenching as he speaks.

"Cleo." His words spill out in a whisper. "I want to—I want to hear everything. I want to understand and apologize until I run out of words, but Graves is far worse than what happened to you."

"You're only just figuring that out now?" I murmur.

"I mean my sister just told me why they're here. You remember the very first thing we did on the bridge?"

"Take your clothes off?" I offer, but my smile is weak. It still draws an answering twitch from him.

"Believe me, I noticed that. We tried to send out a message, so we could get Orbital to override the systems and save us, because nobody else could. You said it yourself—Pax can override any system on Mars."

My insides swoop like I'm falling. "Hunter, who's your sister about to screw?"

He looks like he's in pain. "They're going to use the UN

register to remotely access some of the smaller colonies and settlements. They're going to blow their seals and take them out, make it look like it was caused by a malfunction here at Pax, when this base blows up. Graves always leaves back doors in our software—Marguerite can hide her tracks."

"Even the smallest colonies—that would kill hundreds of people, maybe thousands. Why would they do that?"

"To claim the territory, and all resources there, because technically once everyone's dead, they'll be abandoned."

"They can't," I breathe, a low knot of horror in my gut assuring me that they absolutely can.

Hunter shakes his head slowly. "And if the deaths aren't enough, this will turn Mars into a battlefield. Everyone will suspect Graves, and they'll start their own land grabs. It'll be chaos."

It's like cold water is trickling down my spine as I imagine the future he's painting. Imagine the raids, the attacks on the innocent. "I wish I could say I was surprised," I say softly. "I'm horrified, but I'm not surprised."

"I am," Hunter confesses. "And that's on me. I think I understand, now, why my father pulled away from it all, buried himself in his art. I bought into what it meant to be a Graves, but I think he saw the truth of it. He shouldn't have run, though. He should have stayed to fight. Tried to make us something better."

"That's not always easy," I murmur.

Hunter doesn't reply. His arms are still around me, his body against mine in case Nico's watching, but the hand pressed against my back has curled into a fist.

And though he doesn't say it, I know what he's asking. Slowly, realization is creeping through me.

If we're going to do anything about this, it will take both of us. And we have to know what we're sacrificing—we have to look it in the eye, or we'll falter when it matters.

He'll be giving up any hope of finding a place in his family. Of leading this company that changed the world, that he's been so proud of. He'll be giving up his sister, after he only just found her again.

I'll be giving up my last chance to live a quiet life. I'll be giving up the chance to stop running for the first time.

Though probably neither of us will make it out of this alive, so none of that will matter.

And for both of us, it will mean trusting someone again. It will mean leaning into the kind of bond that's hurt us over and over, as everyone we've ever loved has let us down.

But though it might be too late—too late to help, too late to trust—I have to try. With Hunter, and for Hunter, and for every innocent out there who doesn't deserve to have Graves do what they did to me—destroy their lives.

"I don't suppose you have a plan," I say slowly.

Hunter shakes his head, eyes still closed. "Not even the start of one. Just trying to go up against them is incredibly stupid. But I know who I want to be in this corner with, Cleo. I wouldn't leave it—I wouldn't leave you—even if I could."

I reach up to cup his cheek and I wait until his lashes lift and his steady green gaze meets mine. It's full of pain, but unflinching.

"This might be who GravesUP is," I say softly. "But it's not who you are, Hunter. I know that." And I do, I'm realizing. I know it in my bones. He's shown me who he is at every turn, with every choice he's made.

"I was so wrong," he murmurs. "I believed . . ."

I lift up on my toes and brush his lips with mine, and sparks explode inside me. He falls silent, save for a soft sound in the back of his throat that's pretty gratifying, if I'm honest. "You already said you were wrong about Graves," I whisper. "You're here now, that's what matters."

"No," he replies. "I was wrong about *you*. My sister's broken the rules for the worst kinds of reasons. If you've done anything wrong at all, it was out of desperation. I'm sorry I didn't understand that."

I use my grip on the front of his shirt to pull him into me, and then his mouth's on mine, and I let the kiss speak for me as his hand curls through my hair, and the warmth of his body sets mine alight.

When I finally draw back, I let out a slow breath. "You said going up against them would be incredibly stupid? Well, we have maybe an hour and a half left. That's more than enough time to do something stupid."

28.

HUNTER

1 HOUR, 40 MINUTES REMAINING

I WANT TO STAY here in this moment forever, hidden from the rest of the greenhouse by vines, Cleo's arms twined around my neck, her body curved to fit mine. I want to hide from everything except the girl in my arms—press pause on the outside world so we can linger here.

But instead, I make myself focus as she speaks softly in my ear, her breath setting off fireworks underneath my skin.

"We have to get a message out somehow. Can you get access to the system, if your sister trusts you?"

I swallow hard and let myself run my hand down her back as I think. "If I had her cuff, I could do it. I got a look at the displays it was throwing up—I think it'll have a master override. If I had that, I could send a distress signal. I could send out a warning telling the other colonies to cut themselves off from thc UN's outside command channels, turn off their emergency protocols, so nobody could trigger anything remotely."

Cleo's whispering again, and I have to close my eyes to focus on what she's saying. "The best option would be to swap your cuff for hers, instead of stealing hers and leaving her wrist bare. She might not notice right away if we replace it with something, give us some time to send the messages."

"Okay," I murmur, my brain starting to spin back up to full speed. "So how do we get her to take it off voluntarily?"

"And ideally somewhere there won't be a heap of witnesses," Cleo adds. "None of them trust us. Sabrina will do the right thing by me if she can—she's not a killer—but she'll save herself first."

I can't help myself. I drop my head to find the soft skin of her neck, kissing my way down to the place it meets her shoulder. She shivers in my arms, and my breath catches.

"Concentrate," she whispers fiercely, though the hand she lifts to push my head away is half-hearted at best.

"I am," I reply, running one fingertip slowly up her spine.

"On crime," she clarifies.

"I do my best thinking like this," I murmur against her skin.

I can't have found this girl just to lose her.

That can't be how this ends.

29.

CLEO

1 HOUR, 38 MINUTES REMAINING

WHEN WE WALK OUT into the main greenhouse a couple of minutes later, I know my cheeks must be pink. I keep my head down and don't make eye contact with Nico or Grace. I'm glad they didn't send Sabrina with us—she'd read me better.

I take up my place at the control panel again, crouching down and choosing my next circuit to yank out. As I settle into position, I feel Hunter's cuff shift where I've stuffed it down my cleavage.

What? My lower half is still in my pressure suit, and that doesn't come with pockets. A girl's gotta keep her treasures somewhere.

It's hard not to wince as I pull another circuit out. I'm trying to preserve the heat as long as I can—some of the plants won't make it, but if the water doesn't freeze, I might save the fish.

Unless they do blow this whole place up. Then the fish are on their own. The oxygen levels must be pretty high by now.

In fact, I'm kind of counting on that, for what I'm about to do next.

"I think our odds are pretty good," Hunter murmured as he gave me one last kiss.

"And I have questions about what kind of math they taught you at your fancy school," I muttered, but I let him kiss me anyway.

"Please," he said afterward, in a lordly tone. "I had private tutors."

"Rich boy."

He laughed. "You know, you're the only person in my life who seems to like me *less* because I could buy and sell Jerhattan."

"That a problem?"

He smiled, and kissed me one more time. "No. I like your priorities."

Now he's wandering over toward the tomatoes again, closer to Susanna Hirano's desk, all covered in daisies and monitors he knows how to log in to.

I start softly singing Victoriana Lu's finest work to myself as I yank another wire.

Gonna blast into space, baby!

Gonna hit third base, baby!

Gotta love this face, baby!

Rocket to the moon, yeah!

Nico starts to turn to track Hunter, somehow not completely entranced by my performance, and that means I'm out of time. With a quick prayer regarding the oxygen levels in my personal part of the greenhouse, I touch two wires together.

They send up a shower of sparks, and I throw myself backward with maximum drama, as if I've just been shocked.

Agony shoots up my spine and down my arms as I land too hard and I let myself roll around on the ground with real groans, stars dancing between me and the greenery bursting from racks on the roof. That was way more realistic than it needed to be.

"Fire!" Grace shouts, and I roll onto my side to see two pairs of feet charging over. She and Nico stamp out a fire that's sprung to life where a few of the sparks landed on some mulch laid out over a garden bed.

They get it under control in just a few seconds, but that was way too much, too fast—they really have pumped up the O_2 levels.

One pair of boots turns toward me, and I groan again, to make sure their attention stays on me. A boot nudges me in the ribs.

"You okay?" Nico asks, and I flop over onto my back.

"Ow," I moan. "Give me a minute."

"What happened?" he asks, frowning.

"She electrocuted herself," Grace chips in, from somewhere up by my head.

"I shocked myself," I correct her. "Electrocution is what you call it if it kills you. Well, I guess other people call it that. You're not calling it anything, you're dead."

"What happened, though?" Nico insists. "To the system."

"This isn't an exact science," I reply, allowing myself to inject my tone with some extra snark as I carefully lever myself up to sit.

Nico offers me a hand, and I let him pull me to my feet. I limp back over to my station, dragging things out as best I can, and start in on a too-detailed explanation of what I'm going to try next. A minute later I become aware of a third body standing behind me and watching my progress.

Hunter's back. I hope I gave him enough time.

"Those sparks caught quickly," he says to Nico and Grace, conversational.

"Doesn't matter," I offer, right on cue. "If the fire got big enough, the suppressors would have turned on and caught it."

"The suppressors," Grace murmurs behind me. "Right."

A shiver runs down my spine, and I don't know if I manage to hide it. Maybe it's just getting cold in here.

Ten minutes later we're all back at the engineering offices.

Nico strides over to Marguerite for a quiet conversation, and Grace takes me by the shoulder, steering me to a display where we can start looking for more places to reduce power.

Mr. Chin-Up walks by briefly—taking a break from chiseling the Boxer free of his prison, I guess—and he shoots me a look that's pure poison. He could crack my head like a walnut, and he wants me to know it.

"What about this whole wing of living quarters?" I suggest unhelpfully, pointing to an area they'll have to move through if they want to plant charges for their explosions later.

"Mmm, what else you got?" Grace asks, looking up as Marguerite walks over to join us, Hunter a few steps behind her. He's doing well—his body language says he's on her team. He's giving her a hint of deference. Not too much, but following her lead.

Grace steps aside and lets Marguerite lean in to start working her way through our menus. She doesn't pull out the virtual keyboard we've been using—instead she taps her cuff, and it brute-forces a link to the station we've been working at, projecting a larger, more complex screen in the air in front of us. She has menus and submenus available that we couldn't see a moment ago.

I sit back, ignoring the bruises from my performance in the greenhouse, and study Hunter's twin as she works. There's so much about her that's familiar—the line between her eyebrows as she concentrates, just like his. The green of her eyes, flecked with a golden brown, reflecting the bright light of the displays in front of her as she stares at them, unblinking. They have the same jaw, the same hint of a dimple at one corner of their mouth. And yet they're nothing alike.

She flips efficiently through a few screens, her hands shifting subtly through the air like she's conducting a very tiny orchestra, and I fold my own hands in my lap to prevent any outward sign of my inward celebration. This was the reason Nico beelined for her when we came back here—he picked up the hint we laid down about the fire suppressors. She's realized they need to shut all the fire-protection systems down, to be completely sure their blasts take hold when they set them off.

I desperately fight the urge to look at Hunter, and instead focus on sitting silently, looking defeated as Marguerite wrestles with the code. It's hard to turn off major safety features, for obvious reasons. But the system gives up and rolls over after a couple of minutes. I carefully duck my head as she reaches in to execute the final command . . .

. . . and the world turns white.

Massive amounts of sodium bicarbonate powder are dumped from the ceiling vent, ready to put out the electrical fire the system thinks we're caught up in right now. All around me I hear coughing and cursing, see the dark shapes of others moving around me.

She's *activated* the system, not turned it off. *Well done, Hunter Graves*.

I can practically feel his pain, that he can't take credit for that bit of on-the-fly hacking, jammed in at Susanna's greenhouse workstation, while I rolled around on the floor after my shock. I don't think either of us was sure until this moment that he'd successfully reversed the commands.

I can't see a thing except for swirls and puffs of white right now, and someone's hand claps down on my shoulder to keep me in my seat. All around us I hear people coughing, and after a moment I see Marguerite's screen, projected onto the white cloud. Above us, the fans whir as they start to work overtime.

"Is this stuff toxic?" someone calls out.

"It's sodium bicarb," someone else replies. "You can cook with it. It's fine."

This is my cue. "Um . . ." I let reluctance ooze into my voice and pause to be sure I've hooked the people nearest me.

"What?" Marguerite snaps.

"Too much of this stuff can cause, um, digestive issues," I say as delicately as I can manage. "Pretty intense ones."

It's sort of true. True enough.

"You've got to be kidding," Grace mutters, still beside me.

"Unfortunately not," I reply. "But we didn't shut down the water supply yet, so the showers are still available. We should rinse it off, and maybe relocate to the bridge?"

So that's how I end up walking through the silent base at gunpoint, covered head to toe in white powder. Hunter rigged some of the other suppressors to go off as well, so it wouldn't be suspicious that it only happened in the room we were in. He didn't have time to get them all, I guess. Pity—it would have coated the whole station and made blowing it up that much harder.

The showers are in one big, communal room. Floor-to-ceiling walls divide each cubicle, and each one has a curtain you can pull across the front for privacy.

Hunter disappears into one straightaway, already pulling off his shirt to gratuitously show off his excellent back muscles. I absolutely do not think about the way the water will be sluicing down his body in a minute when he showers. Not even a little.

He's left a cubicle free between us, and Marguerite heads into it, firmly drawing the curtain behind her. "Five minutes, people," she calls out, sounding cranky. Which, fair.

A pissed-off Grace, covered in white from head to toe, checks my cubicle to be sure there's nothing useful to a prisoner in there, and then ushers me inside. She stays dressed for now, one hand on her gun.

I catch her eye and pull the curtain across experimentally,

silently asking if I get privacy for this. She nods and takes one step back.

I yank the curtain the rest of the way, and waste no time. I retrieve Hunter's cuff from its hiding place in my cleavage, then haul off my tank and bra. I shimmy my pressure suit down over my hips, dumping my powdery clothes on the bench just inside the cubicle's opening. Then I hit the control panel with my palm, and step into the glorious stream of water.

This moment is almost as good as kissing Hunter. It's like the warmth of the shower washes away not just the white powder and the sweat and the red dust that permanently clings to me, but the fear as well, just for a moment. Something inside me unclenches, and I close my eyes as I tip my face up to the spray, letting myself have this. It might be my last peaceful moment.

I only have a moment, though—I have to hurry, and this next part of the plan has zero finesse. I leave the water running, watching the white gunk drain away toward its date with the water recyc system, which probably isn't going to love it—assuming it continues to exist long enough to form an opinion.

Then I wrap a towel around myself and stick Hunter's cuff down my cleavage again.

Carefully I poke my head out around the curtain, ready with an excuse about the soap dispenser, but Grace is near the door now, talking to her girlfriend, Blue Braid. Which I guess means she's off her table in the classroom, and our enemies are almost up to full strength again. There's something softer in Grace's body language as she looks up toward her lover. *I'm sure glad you didn't get fried*, I'm sure she's saying.

Anyway, she's distracted, which means this is my moment. I carefully lean around the divide between the cubicles and get a look at Marguerite's clothes sitting on her little shelf.

Her cuff sits atop her clothes.

The trick in moments like this is to be quick and decisive. I slide my hand into the gap, closing it on the cuff, my heart trying to hammer its way out of my chest.

I start to pull the cuff free, my other hand lifting to pull Hunter's from its hiding place.

Hopefully she'll just slip on Hunter's cuff, and not notice it's duller than hers. That'll give Hunter a few minutes to try to hack his way through her protections and send out our SOS and our warning.

A hand grabs my shoulder and yanks me back—then the person spins me around and I find myself looking into the furious gaze of Blue Braid.

Oh, shit.

30.

HUNTER

1 HOUR, 15 MINUTES REMAINING

CLEO SCREAMS IN PAIN, and I bolt out of the shower, not even bothering to shut the water off.

I wrap a towel around my waist and hustle out of my cubicle to find Cleo's been grabbed by Blue Braid, who's twisting her arm up behind her back.

Marguerite shows up a moment later, also in a towel, and shoots me a questioning look. I force myself to shrug, force myself to keep my expression neutral, even though my heart rate's surging. Years in the corporate world have at least taught me which mask I need right now.

Blue Braid reaches forward to wrench a cuff from Cleo's hand, then offers it to my sister. Marguerite leans forward to take it slowly, and my heart sinks as I see the shine on it—it's hers.

Marguerite carefully curls it around her wrist and then lifts her gaze to study Cleo. Then she shakes her head. "If she's not prepared to play with us, then get her out of the way," she says crisply.

"Wait," I manage, going cold inside. "Wait, what are you going to—"

"Get it together," Marguerite snaps, rolling her eyes. "Nobody's shooting your girlfriend. But if you think we're taking her with us, you're insane."

Her gaze is directly on me now, and the moment draws out between us, tension mounting as she waits for my reply.

She's testing me—she's looking for a sign I'm on her side, or a sign I'm on Cleo's.

A storm passes through me in less than a millisecond—sharp fear for Cleo, fury at my sister, rage at my own helplessness—and then everything stills.

I dig deep and find the Graves in me—find every part of me that knows how to be a shark, that could die of blood loss before I let my wounds show—and I hold up a hand. "No, I get it," I say easily. "Whatever that was, it was . . . I mean, she's a criminal. I met her a few hours ago, and fun's fun, but I'm not going to fight you to keep her. But we're not done yet, we're short on time, and she knows the station."

Part of me is numb, and part of me is still roaring with anger and despair, deep inside, like a wound's opening that I don't think will ever heal. This could be our last conversation. These could be the last words Cleo hears me speak. *How can I do this to her?*

"Fuck you," Cleo spits, struggling against Blue Braid's grip, and the words go through me like a knife. "I'd rather die than stand here with you. All the Graves family has ever done is screw over anyone they can find with less power than them. You're barely human. If you leave me behind—if I'm not a part of your murder machine—then that's an honor."

My lungs are so tight I can't make myself draw a breath. *Cleo, I'm sorry. I'm so sorry.*

Marguerite looks at Cleo blankly for a long moment and then rolls her eyes again. "God, the drama," she mutters. "Will someone get her out of my sight?"

Cleo wrenches free of Blue Braid suddenly, throwing herself at me, wrapping her arms around my neck, and suddenly my world is all wet girl and towel and desperation. "Hunter," she gasps, clinging to me. "Don't let them take me! I'm sorry! I don't want to die!"

Something cracks inside me and I start to shift, start to wrap my arm around her—and then she staggers back from me, as though I've pushed her.

"The hell with you," she spits, wet hair falling around her face.

She's cementing my position. She's making it look like I just rejected her. She's spending her last moments with me trying to keep me safe—trying to make sure I survive this screwup, that I can keep fighting.

So I lift my chin and do the only thing I can, to honor what she's giving me. "Find her a pair of pants and get her out of here," I tell Blue Braid, taking a step back and securing my own towel more carefully around my waist. And then, to Marguerite: "What did she even think she was going to do with a cuff? She doesn't know the first thing about coding."

I can't help marveling at the note of almost . . . boredom in my tone. It's like I'm outside myself, watching this happen, helpless to stop it. I'm trapped by the thousands of hostages out there who don't even know they're in danger. The innocent people who'll die if I don't keep trying. If I don't let them take away Cleo, to keep myself safe.

Blue Braid marches Cleo along the row of cubicles and out the door.

I fold my arms across my chest, forcing myself to remain in place as I watch every last second of her, drinking her in until the moment she's gone.

Only then do I realize that my own cuff is back around my wrist.

That was the other reason she threw herself at me. My heart clenches. *Cleo*.

"Let's keep moving," says Marguerite, snapping into motion. "Nico, go prep the rovers for departure. Everyone else, let's get dressed—you know your jobs."

Nico's just arrived with armfuls of clothes salvaged from nearby living quarters, and he makes his way along to offer each of us the best of what he's got.

"No problem," he says, handing Marguerite a fresh shirt. "I'll get them prepped." But there's a question in his eyes that I don't understand, even though I sense the weight of it. He's asking her something that goes deeper than he's saying.

Marguerite gives him a don't-fuck-with-me look in return. "Hunter will ride with me," she says quietly, and he nods.

As we duck back into our cubicles to change, I linger long enough to retrieve Cleo's specially modified headset when nobody's looking. I'd rather be untraceable, whatever happens next.

What was that exchange between Nico and Marguerite just now? What did that look he gave her mean? Was Nico challenging my sister?

My heart is still in pieces—I'm still reeling—but if something just happened, and it's a place I can drive a wedge between them, then I have to figure out what it was.

Our lives might depend on it.

58 MINUTES REMAINING

I'm sticking to the shadows and watching Nico as he works his way through the rovers the Graves team arrived in. There are three, and he's on the second now.

I'm a software guy, not a hardware guy, and it takes me a minute to figure out what he's doing—but then it clicks. He's getting into the guts of each one and he's disconnecting things.

Realization slowly creeps over me, shock taking over from the pain of watching them haul Cleo away.

Nico is leaving exactly one lifeboat still functioning. That's why my sister told him I'll be in hers. Because the others won't start at all.

I don't know why I'm surprised. She came here prepared to kill thousands of people from other settlements—why wouldn't she wipe out her own team? If she takes them with her, they're a vulnerability, each one a potential leak. I asked her about her crew. I asked her if they'd be a liability. *Don't worry about them*, she said.

Eventually, no matter what kind of explosion takes this place out, someone's going to work out there are bodies here that shouldn't be here, and extra rovers docked. It'll take a while, though, and everything—the uniforms, the rovers, their equipment—is unmarked. It was the first thing I noticed when they arrived. She's been planning this since the start.

These people work with her. She knows their names. And she has Nico prepping to leave them behind.

Nico straightens up, stretches his back, and walks around to check the controls of the rover, tapping at the screen as he brings up the displays. Doesn't want the sabotage to be too obvious too soon, I guess.

I hold my position, trying to slow my thoughts. I don't have long before I'm due back—I told Marguerite I wanted to check Cleo's work in the greenhouse. I said nobody had been watching her closely enough. She could have tried to sabotage it. It's a thin excuse, but my sister's busy.

I slowly ease back along the balcony and out through a door, into a quiet passage.

Shock is giving way to a strange kind of calm. Everything's narrowing down to the next fifty-five minutes of my life.

Thousands of people out there are relying on me, even if they have no idea. Cleo's relying on me.

I treat this moment like a programming problem—I close my eyes, cast out my thoughts, and take in the whole of the picture. I let the facts run through my brain without hooking on to any one thing, like a cascade of numbers falling in front of me as I scan them for the combination I need.

I need a weakness. I need a place where I can find a crack and start to pull it open.

Is it one of her people? Is it one of her systems? Is it . . . wait.

Wait.

Slowly, for the first time in what feels like forever, I start to smile.

Because I know what to do.

53 MINUTES REMAINING

Sabrina's striding quickly as she makes her way back from the oxygenators, where she's been making the last adjustments to the oxygen flow. We won't feel the effects for hours—and this place doesn't have hours, but the levels must be so high by now that the smallest spark . . .

I step out in front of her as she reaches an intersection, and she stops immediately, wary.

"We have to talk," I say quietly. "And fast, I'm expected back."

Her eyes narrow and she looks me up and down, assessing.

"Oh," she says, after a moment. "Not so close with your sister after all, huh? Don't do this for Cleo. I'm sorry about it too, but she was stupid and this is what happens when you're stupid. You don't have to be, and I'm sure not going to be."

"I get it," I reply, holding up both hands, keeping my tone easy. I'm a Graves. I know how to stay calm during a negotiation. "You've picked a side."

"I've picked the side that pays me," she replies.

"Here's the thing, though." I pause, let the tension kick up a notch. "That side you've picked? It hasn't picked you back."

She frowns. "Say what?"

I take a step closer. "You'll have to figure out how to verify this on your own, but I've just seen Nico disabling two of your three rovers. You think you're getting a ride in my sister's? That she's going to haul a loose end like you on out of here?"

Sabrina studies me. "She's taking you, I'm guessing," she says.

"I mean, maybe," I agree. "Seems that way for now, but who knows."

Sabrina's staring at me steadily now, trying to figure me out. She's sizing me up in the way her world has taught her to. "Why are you telling me about the rovers when you've got a place on one?" she asks.

I answer her question with a question. "Cleo told me you're not a killer. I'm trying to figure it out—was she wrong, or do you really not know what my sister's doing here?"

"Look," she says, shaking her head. "I don't care what games you corporates play with each other."

"I don't think you know what the game is," I say quietly. This is where the risk lies, in this one moment—this is the question that everything hinges on. Cleo thinks there's some good in Sabrina. It's time to see if she's right.

Sabrina doesn't take the bait—but she doesn't walk away either. Instead she just stares at me, so I keep going.

"Marguerite's not here for corporate espionage," I say. "She's not just grabbing data from the UN servers. She's going to remotely blow up six different settlements. Thousands of people will die, and when nobody's left, the settlements will be declared abandoned. Then Graves will roll in and claim them."

Sabrina's lips part in shock, her eyes widening as she absorbs what I've just told her. But what she *doesn't* do is contradict me. It's all too easy to believe.

"Do you really think she's prepared to do that, and *not* prepared to leave you for dead?" I press. "You're a liability."

"How do I know you're telling the truth?" she whispers.

"Check the rovers. If two are disabled, then you know. You'll have to trust me on her plans."

Sabrina's perfectly still for a moment, and she reminds me of Cleo, the way she pauses to size up her new situation, to assess, to look for the next place to leap to. She's thinking furiously, calculating. "I thought this was just rich folks screwing with each other," she murmurs.

"It's not," I say. "And I think this is way past what you signed on for. I don't think you want those deaths on your conscience any more than I do."

Her whole body is still, her muscles rigid, her gaze fixed

somewhere past me as she absorbs what I'm telling her. Weighs it up against who she believes herself to be. What she believes my sister capable of. I can only hope desperately that Cleo was right about her.

"There's no way to get a signal out to warn the other bases," I say. "Not without Marguerite's cuff, and Cleo failed at getting that. But if we can get a rover close enough to the nearest base, we could broadcast a short-range message."

Sabrina lifts her chin a little, and now she's beginning to understand why I'm telling her all this.

"I'm betting they've taken your handprint off the authorization list," I say. "But I can get inside the code and put it back, so you can get the remaining rover started."

"Why not just add yours?" she asks. And then she laughs, a quick bark, lifting one hand to pinch the bridge of her nose. "You can't drive it, can you?"

"I can't drive it," I agree. "Not on unfamiliar terrain, in the tail end of a dust storm. Today isn't the day for me to learn. And anyway, my handprint isn't registered anywhere in the system. It would take too long to get it in there. Yours, I just need to connect back to the rover authorization list."

She nods slowly.

I risk a question: "Do you need to take a look at the rovers, confirm what I'm telling you?"

She's quiet a long moment, and I see her run through everything again—pull up everything she knows, and see the way it clicks together.

"No," she says grimly. "I believe you."

"Then I need you to go buy me a few minutes by distracting my sister while I put you back on the rover's permission list," I say. "Tell her you saw me and I was on my way back."

"Sure. What then?"

"Then a number of things have to happen in exactly the right order, or we both die here."

She lets out a breath. "Talk. I'm listening."

31.

CLEO

40 MINUTES REMAINING

I DON'T KNOW IF I'm being walked to prison, or my execution, and I'm not sure if there's a difference.

Blue Braid has me at gunpoint, and we're making our way past the living quarters in silence as I frantically run through everything I know, everything I've learned, trying to come up with *anything* that could save me.

I don't think it's going to work, though. I'm realizing with a kind of dull surprise that I'm out of ideas. I think this is it.

Then Sabrina steps out into the path ahead of us, gun in hand, and I stop. She's grim, her jaw squared, her lips pressed into a thin line.

"I'll take her," she says quietly.

"I've got it," Blue Braid replies from behind me. "The boss said—"

Sabrina shakes her head—a quick, sharp movement. "I vouched for her," she says. "It's my responsibility."

My mouth goes dry, my throat closing. Holy shit, this is actually it. My breath's shaking as it rasps in and out of lungs I can't seem to fill. *Hunter, where are you?*

Except I don't want him to come—even though I selfishly want him with me, I need him to stay with Marguerite. I need him to stay and fight for the thousands of people we're trying to save. And I'm praying he's strong enough to choose them, not me.

Blue Braid pushes past me, and for an instant I consider lunging for her gun. But Sabrina's weapon is pointed straight at me, and I force myself to stay still.

"Your call," Blue Braid says, shrugging. She claps Sabrina on the shoulder and heads around the curve of the hallway.

Sabrina and I stay right where we are as she disappears out of sight. I'm running through every delaying tactic in the book and coming up empty—she'll know them all for what they are.

Then Sabrina holsters her gun. "We don't have a lot of time," she says. "Let's go."

I spin around, my mouth open as she strides off in the opposite direction to Blue Braid. She doesn't slow her pace, though, and I jog behind her, scrambling to understand.

"Sabrina, what's happening?"

"Keep up. We're heading for the rovers."

"I . . . what? Marguerite's decided to take me with her?"

Sabrina snorts. "You're not that stupid."

We make our way into the empty garage, and Sabrina heads straight for the parking bay on the right. The rover there is sitting in its airlock, the two doors in front and behind it sealed shut.

"The other two are disabled," she says quietly. "The only people who were meant to get out of here were Marguerite Graves and Nico—and then possibly your boyfriend, once he showed up."

Shock ripples through my body as I absorb what she's saying. And then I understand. "Hunter told you what's happening."

"He sure did," she replies. "Now let's pray he can dance like he promised." She presses her hand to the garage door, and her shoulders sag with relief as it opens.

I follow her inside, stepping out of the way as she swings the door of the rover open and climbs in to begin the start-up sequence. "How far away is Hunter?" I ask as I climb into the back to leave a front seat for him.

Sabrina shoots me a look I can't read, though it's not patient, and fishes off her headset, passing it to me. "He's on channel one," she says. "I made sure the others aren't there, told them it kept getting bursts of static, so they're over on three. You can talk without them listening."

I tune it quickly, pulling my harness into place. "Hey, hurry up," I say, hoping Hunter's listening. "We're ready."

It's a moment before his reply arrives, crystal clear in my ear—as if he's right behind me, so close I could touch him.

Cleo, he murmurs. He's speaking low—I can hear other voices behind him, and the sounds of monitors throwing up alerts. *Cleo, I'm . . . You need to go right now, and send a warning message as soon as you can.*

"But how will you . . . ?" And then my heart clenches, because I already know the answer.

For a moment I'm perfectly still, refusing to acknowledge it, refusing to even let myself *think* it. There's a strange ringing in my ears and everything around me seems far away.

Hunter won't get out. He's given the last working rover to me. He's getting *me* out. He's found a way to choose me *and* the thousands of people at stake—but only at the cost of himself. He's going to die here.

Everything roars back to life around me as that knowledge settles—as if the sound and the color of the world just got turned back up.

"Hunter," I gasp. "Hunter, no, you can't."

Up front, Sabrina hits the command for the door seals and they swing closed. "No!" I clamber into the front seat to grab for the handle. But as my fingers close on it, the whole parking bay lights up red. It's depressurizing to match the atmosphere of the planet outside—and I'm not wearing a suit.

I'm trapped in this rover.

The door behind us rises to reveal Mars beyond it, and then we're backing out.

Sobs roll through me, my throat constricting as if someone's got their hand around it and they're squeezing unbearably hard. "Hunter, please," I gasp. "She'll kill you."

His voice comes back quiet, calm. *There are thousands of*

people depending on us. Every second counts. Send the message as soon as you get in range, all right? Make them hear you, whatever it takes.

Tears spill down my cheeks. I'm working toward being a crying, snotty mess, but this is a short-range radio and I'm going to lose him in a moment. The only person who's ever truly put himself on the line for me.

He didn't leave me when my suit breached, and he's still not leaving me.

Hunter could be in this rover. He could have run with Sabrina, but he chose my safety above his. He chose me.

A lifetime of lessons in trusting nobody but myself, and finally I've found the one person I could break that rule for. The one person I *can* trust. Only to lose him.

This is a boy who deserves my heart, and too late I realize I should have given it to him when I had the chance. Because now he's slipping through my fingers, and there's no way to grab him.

In this moment I'd choose Hunter's life over a thousand others, but I can't. Sabrina's turning the rover away from the doors that are already closing behind us.

"Hunter," I manage, tearing the words from my throat. "I'd have come all the way to Mars just to find this. To find *you*."

But the only response is a soft static hiss. We're out of range.

The rover is silent then, except for my sobs. It's a full minute before Sabrina speaks. "He could be sitting right where you are now. He made me promise to get you instead. We're going to make what he's doing worth it."

"Yes," I manage, trying to blink the tears away from my eyes.

She's gazing straight ahead, eyes narrowed in concentration. "They'll have seen the doors opening," she says. "They'll be after us as soon as they can restore another rover, and the visibility out here is shit. So sit your ass down, bring up the nav system, and plot us a course. We don't have time to drive around a crater we could have avoided, or reverse out of a field of rubble."

And through the muffling numbness, I make myself move, reaching out for the controls to bring up the nav display. It springs to life, projected against the windshield, superimposing the map over the barely visible landscape around us. The lights blur against my tears.

We're going to get within range of *someone* we can warn. It might be the last thing we're able to do.

In fact, I don't care if it *is* the last thing I do.

I can't imagine what could ever come after this.

32.

HUNTER

31 MINUTES REMAINING

***I'd have come all** the way to Mars just to find this. To find* you.

"Cleo, I—" But there's only a static hiss. She's gone. My heart's racing, but I feel strangely empty, as though some piece of me has been lifted out and all that's left is echoes.

I'm standing on the bridge with my sister and most of her crew—I've been murmuring into my mic, my hand up to guard my mouth—and as I turn back toward them, Marguerite's head snaps up.

"Why did a rover just depart?" she raps out, and everyone turns toward her like they're tracking the sun.

Nico just takes off at a run, disappearing through the door in a blur of movement, and I hustle over to my sister, pulling up a display from my cuff.

"Who was it?" I ask her urgently, because anything that buys even a second's distraction is worth it.

She's pulling up displays at lightning speed, and in a moment she'll figure out someone added Sabrina's handprint permission back into the rover list. I try to look as if I'm helping, getting in the midst of it with her, yanking code just as she touches it, and making as much of a mess as I possibly can without giving myself away any sooner than I have to.

Then, with a flourish, I overload the system enough to bounce us both out. "What the—" I mutter a false protest, throwing my hands up. "The power's failing, everything's breaking down."

Marguerite curses as she starts all over again, so I dive back in alongside her.

My thoughts are racing across the red planet outside, chasing after the tiny rover crawling across its surface. *Cleo, run!*

I don't care what it costs me—I just want her out of here. Yes, to warn people, of course to warn people. But more than that, because I want to know she's out there *living*. That her smile and her sarcasm and her quick wits are out there somewhere on Mars, with another chance at life.

I should have said that, instead of going on about sending a message she already knew was urgent. But I missed my chance.

I hope one day she figures out what I really meant.

When Marguerite left, I told myself that if loving people made you vulnerable, it wasn't worth the risk.

Something broke in me then, and hardened instead of healing, I brought up my shields. But that was never the right way. The answer wasn't to become more *like* my sister.

It was to become more *than* her.

And that's what's happened, with Cleo. I've learned it's

worth the risk, to leap. That a trust fall can kill you, sure, but it can save you too.

Whatever happens next, Cleo's saved a part of me. And now I'm going to go down trying to save her.

Marguerite's back in the code again, cursing softly as she tries to figure out what's going on, and I lean across to her.

"Should I go help Nico?" I murmur. "Maybe I can do more on-site."

It's a risk, this moment—she hasn't actually told me they disabled the other rovers, but I'm hoping she won't remember that, now I've got her flustered. And sure enough, she just nods.

"Go," she says, soft enough that nobody else will hear it. "Get a rover ready for us. The solar's almost completely gone now and we have maybe ten minutes left before your girlfriend's into range to send a warning. I need to make sure there's nobody there to receive it."

I go cold all over.

She's not in the code to try to figure out how Cleo and Sabrina got away, how Sabrina got her handprint back on the permissions list.

She's moving up the time of the bombings, so their warning will be useless. Cleo would have had twenty-five minutes to get her message out. Now she's got ten. And she doesn't know.

"Can I help with that?" I ask, scrambling for a new plan. I need her to let me in if I'm going to slow her down.

"I've got it," Marguerite replies. "I built it, I can wrestle it. There's no time to catch you up." She spares me a glance then, reaching across to squeeze my shoulder, and lowers her voice even further. "Get us a ride out of here, brother."

There's an ache in me, for what my sister could have been to me—what she *should* have been to me. For what she's not.

I reach up to hook Cleo's headset over my ear and start my jog toward the rover garages.

I duck into a side passageway as soon as I'm out of sight, and then another, and wrench open the door to someone's quarters so I can slip inside.

I try to pull the door closed behind me, but it sticks—it's the failing power. As the station dies, it's meant to start leaving doors open so nobody gets trapped.

I give up, stumbling over to sit on one of the bunks. I'm breathing hard, sweating now, my heart pounding.

I only have a couple of minutes before Marguerite figures out I never reached Nico. Can I get into the system and undo her detonation orders in that time?

No. She's right, she built it. I can't force my way in and unravel all her code in the next few minutes. I need another angle.

I need to distract her enough that she can't speed up her plans. *Think, Hunter. What would Cleo do?*

Cleo would go for the vital systems, find something that threatens Marguerite herself, so that she *has* to stop and do something about it.

I flick up the display from my cuff and dive into the code one more time, pushing past numbers, chasing something I can use quickly. Then I see it.

I set off the air-quality alarms on the bridge, so the whole space fills with a deafening *WHOOP, WHOOP, WHOOP* that I can hear even from this distance.

Hunter! Marguerite's barely audible over comms. *Get into the controls. Get me some air!*

"I can't," I shout back. "I don't have access. You'll have to do it!"

I lurk in the back of the life-support system as she tries to silence the alarm, listening to her swear over the headset. It takes her longer, because she thinks the alarm is legit. It's another minute she hasn't spent speeding up her timeline—I'll take it.

Then she tags me, finding me where she's working and bumping me out of the life-support sections. Suddenly my display fritzes in front of me and disappears.

I thought you couldn't get in, she snaps over comms.

I'm silent a moment too long, before I find a reply. "It's your air, I kept trying. I'll head for Nico."

She doesn't reply.

Cleo, run faster.

I reset my cuff and start again—what else can I do? Cut power to the bridge? It's so protected, but maybe . . .

And then my sister's voice sounds in my ear again, as she comes back on comms. *You know, Hunter . . .* The hair on the back of my neck stands up at her tone. *What* did *your little friend think she was going to do with my cuff? You said it yourself—she knows nothing about code. Was she going to give it to someone who does know what to do?*

Oh, shit.

I look up to find Nico in the open doorway.

He lunges for me, where I sit on the bed. I throw myself across the room, out of his way. He moves like a fighter, and I might be fit, but I'm not that.

"Come on, now," he says softly, hands spreading wide as he stalks across the room toward me. "Game's over." I can hear the soft buzz of Marguerite's voice in his earpiece, and I flick through the channels on mine to catch the last of her words.

—him quickly.

I edge around the tiny room as Nico turns toward me, shifting to block the path to the door. Fumbling behind me, I run my hand along a shelf, searching desperately for anything I can use as a weapon.

The hell with it, shoot him, Marguerite snaps. *He's picked a side.*

"You don't want to do that," I tell Nico. My fingers reach the end of the shelf and find a flat panel fixed to the wall.

"No?" he asks, sounding a lot like he *does* want to shoot me. He's not drawing his gun, though. Not yet.

"You don't want to shoot a Graves," I point out.

Nico shrugs. "I'm warming up to the idea."

"She's lost it, you know that. You know these aren't orders you should follow. There's barely a way out of this now, but if you kill me . . ."

Nico lunges again, and an instant later I'm pressed up against the wall, his forearm across my throat, cutting off my air. "Who's going to know she gave orders?" he murmurs, eyes meeting mine. "Or that I followed them? Terrible that you died when the station vented."

And now he reaches for his gun.

Black starts to creep in around the edges of my vision, and I wrench at his forearm with one hand, scrabbling behind me with the other. My fingers find the edge of the panel fixed to the wall again.

They're easy to pull out. It's Cleo's voice, back at the engineering offices, making excuses for heading to the greenhouse in person. *They were thinking about maintenance, not sabotage.*

Just have to watch for the live ones.

My vision's going black, my throat spasming at the lack of air.

I dig my fingertips in and wrench off the access panel, reaching inside to grab a handful of wires. Then I yank them free and jam them against Nico's chest.

In a shower of sparks he goes flying backward, crashing into the wall opposite. The lights flicker and go out, plunging us into darkness, and I shove myself at where I think the door was—already there are flames leaping to life where the sparks fell on the bedding.

I ricochet off the frame and stumble out into the hallway, where the emergency lights flicker once and then die.

Nico's somewhere behind me, roaring a curse, so still alive, I guess.

I start sprinting toward the one source of light I can see, a glow around the corner. I need a new hiding place before Nico gets back onto his feet.

I pound down the hallway, swinging around a corner to find an intersection lit by one failing overhead light.

I've been here before. I'm by a familiar stack of crates, with the signs pointing at all the different settlements nearby. Suddenly the numbers feel impossibly large.

Cleo, run!

I duck down behind the boxes as Nico's footsteps sound behind me, trying to keep my ragged breathing as soft as I can. He stumbles into the intersection thirty seconds later, looking as furious as . . . well, as a guy who just got a bunch of live wires jammed into his ribs and was nearly set on fire in a high-oxygen atmosphere.

"Where are you?" he mutters, studying each hallway off the intersection in turn, as I stay crouched behind my boxes.

"Nico!" It's Blue Braid, dressed in a pressure suit, with a helmet under one arm. "Rover, let's go!"

Without another word he abandons the chase, turning to follow her toward the garages. She must have gotten one working again.

Cleo, RUN.

I need to get back to slowing my sister down. I pull up my display from my cuff again, readying myself to plunge back into the station systems and find something to break.

It takes me a moment to understand why the bright lights projected in front of me don't look right.

The air's hazy.

I get to my feet, staggering—my body's hitting the point of exhaustion—and see a stream of smoke snaking its way down the hallway. There's a faint glow visible in the next corner: the direction from which Nico and I came.

Oh, come on. I haven't been through enough?

Above me, fire alarms start to wail mournfully, drawn out and weird, like their batteries are failing. *Fire, fire*, says a woman's annoyingly calm voice, dipping and elongating as the power fluctuates. *Fire, evacuate.*

Okay, so that's on me. And the oxygen levels are high enough now that everything around me could go up in a minute, which means it's time to run again.

I push myself to a jog, hurrying through the dying station until I leave the fire warnings behind. I crouch in what looks like a classroom—it's decorated with kids' drawings and educational charts.

It's also one of the few rooms that has a window port, so I can see the red dust storm outside through the circle of clear material. Maybe it's supposed to be educational for the students, or maybe kids have a special right to sunlight, I don't know.

I sit my tired self down beside the porthole and reach out for my sister on comms. I don't even know what I'm going to say, but anything that distracts her will do.

"So, Marguerite. Was this a cry for attention? Did you suggest this to Mom so she'd finally give you that favorite-child trophy?"

Don't you dare, she snaps back, instantly angry in my ear. *I trusted you. I invited you in.*

"To murder club!" I sputter, pausing to lean against the porthole for a second. Maybe the dust is clearing—I caught a glimpse of the landscape for a moment, red dirt stretching away into the distance.

I pray Cleo's still out there in a rover, racing for safety.

This is the frontier, Marguerite says in my ear. *You have to take what's yours.*

My next words come before I know I'm going to speak them. "That was never what we believed."

It was never what you *believed,* she counters. *You needed the noble speeches to hide behind—you were never brave enough to look what you were doing in the eye and own the fact that you were saving yourself because you* deserved *to be saved. You look down on the rest of us, but at least we knew what this was.*

"That's not true! Marguerite, please. We said that we had to dream huge dreams, and make hard choices, but it was always meant to be for something greater than us."

There is nothing great here without us! she snaps.

"I don't agree," I say. "I'm sitting here in this classroom, looking at these pictures stuck to the wall, thinking about the kids who made them. About who those kids could grow up to be. What they could do for this place, given a chance. Trying to understand how my own sister is willing to murder the children at half a dozen different stations."

She doesn't reply. Instead, the alarm above me starts up again. *Decompression warning,* says the woman, her voice slowing and deepening as the power bleeds away. *Evacuate. Decompression warning.*

"Marguerite!" I shout, but I'm moving, throwing myself off the desk and out the door. I swing around to slap at the palm plate, praying there's enough juice left for the door to close.

It wheezes shut, and through the clear screen that's supposed to let parents watch their children learn, I see the porthole blow, and the school supplies fly up in a flurry of white as the classroom decompresses.

I told her where I was. I'm a fool. But I'm not foolish enough to say anything now—to scream at her, like the anger burning inside me wants to do. Perhaps she won't be able to tell the door closed. Perhaps she'll think I was on the wrong side of it.

Should have come with me, Hunter, she whispers to my ghost.

I can hear alarms wailing in the distance and fire alerts starting to go off. The station's dying around me.

Cleo's not the only person running out of time. The station isn't going to make it to the end of our countdown. That timeline never planned for us running around trying to destroy each other, shorting circuits and setting fires, sabotaging basic functions.

Any second now, fire is going to rip through the oxygen-enriched air and start blowing the seals that protect the base from the outside. The fire will make it a long way in just a few seconds—and then when the seals blow, Pax will decompress.

There's nothing more I can do for Cleo—I have to hope she and Sabrina can stay ahead of Nico and Blue Braid for long enough to deliver their message. Maybe long enough to reach safety, even.

But the thought of Cleo out there on the red planet's surface has given me one last idea, and maybe I have enough time to pull it off.

One last chance at maybe, just maybe . . .

I start to run.

33.

CLEO

12 MINUTES REMAINING

WE'RE ON THE CUSP of radio contact when we see the other rover behind us. The dust storm is still swirling in the air, which means they can't be more than a hundred meters away.

"Shit." I twist around from my nav duties to get a look at them. "How did they catch up?"

"Nico's driving," Sabrina replies, eyes never leaving the path ahead. "He's good. Very good. Plus, they know the way. Take your pick. What do you see?"

"There's nobody in the passenger seat," I say. "But the rover . . . it's the wrong shape." I'm squinting through the haze, trying to make out more details. Then, a chill going through me, I understand. I let out a slow breath that's half a moan.

"Cleo?" Sabrina prompts me, her voice rising.

"He's got someone on the outside," I rasp.

"What now?" She tries to twist her head around, and the rover wobbles, which snaps her attention straight ahead again.

"There's someone on the hood of the rover," I say.

"But why?"

I can see it more clearly now—someone in a pressure suit and helmet. I catch a glimpse of color inside the helmet. It's Blue Braid, with her augmented vision.

She raises her hand, pointing it at us through the fading dust storm.

"So they can shoot at us," I whisper. Neither Sabrina nor I has a pressure suit on—if she puts a hole in the rover, that's the end.

Sabrina hisses between her teeth. "The gloves are pretty slim, but I don't know if she could get her finger through the trigger. Maybe—"

PANG! A bullet ricochets off the rover and we both scream.

"She definitely can!" I screech, slamming down in the seat beside Sabrina again and reaching for the radio one more time.

"African Union, come in, repeat, African Union, come in. This is an emergency transmission, do you read?"

I twist my head to look back—the other rover is closer now. I can see Blue Braid taking aim.

"African Union, come *in*!" I shout down the radio, as if they'll hear me with extra volume.

Then, suddenly, a voice fills the cabin. *Emergency transmission, African Union reads you, but barely. Identify and proceed.*

I hadn't even thought about what I'd say at this point. I just plunge in.

"We're coming from Pax. Be advised, Pax Station has been

taken over by a hostile force. They're going to use the keys from the UN registers to remotely breach your seals and take out your life support. They're targeting multiple bases. You need to cut off all commands from the outside, shut down those pathways, and tell others to do the same. Quickly!"

There's a silence so long, I think I've lost them again—or maybe they've just freaked out, and immediately flicked their comms to the off position. Then the voice finally crackles to life again. *Rover, did you say our life support? You said Pax?*

"Confirm." I'm barely keeping myself from screaming into the radio. My whole body's pins and needles, just waiting for the instant the rover breaches—because I'll only know it for a few seconds and then I'll be done. "Pax has been taken over by a hostile force. Do not hail them. Repeat, do not hail them."

Rover . . . Again, a pause. *Rover, Pax is gone.*

Beside me, Sabrina lets out a groan. "We're going to die catching these guys up," she mutters.

"Not everyone," I reply. "The base evacuated, but there are still personnel on-site."

They can't be, the voice replies. *Rover, I don't mean the people are gone. I mean* Pax *itself is gone.*

Time seems to slow down. A lifetime passes as I turn to look at Sabrina. Her lips part in shock, her eyes widening, and I swear I can feel my heart thumping against the inside of my ribs. "What do you mean, *gone*?"

We have no visuals due to the dust storm, but our satellites are picking up a massive heat signature, the voice from the Afro base replies. *Best guess, the whole base has blown.*

I can't speak. I can't breathe. A shudder goes through me.

Hunter, no.

Beside me, Sabrina swears softly, and the radio crackles again.

Rover, we're sending a party out to meet you and escort you in. ETA, two minutes.

I lift my head, my eyes swimming with tears, and see Nico's rover turn away to carve a new path across the red landscape, maybe to where Graves troops are waiting for an invasion that won't happen. He's missed his chance and he knows it.

"I'm sorry," Sabrina whispers. "At least Marguerite went up before she had a chance to take anyone else with her."

But I can't speak, my throat is closed. Was it Hunter? Did he blow the base up to stop his sister? Did the systems overload early? We should have had another ten minutes before the charges went off.

We should have had ten more minutes.

But it doesn't matter. He's gone.

He's gone.

34.

CLEO

1 HOUR LATER

SABRINA'S SINGING LIKE A canary, explaining exactly what the Graves crew were up to.

"Listen," she's saying to the assembled crowd of stressed-out West African Union staff, one of whom is carefully recording the whole thing. "I thought we were committing a small crime, I'll own up to that. I thought we were yanking some data that would help Graves on the business front. Getting a few hitcher names on the register was part of my payment, and the rest was cash. I did *not* know we were committing wholesale murder. I want that on the record."

She's sitting on one of the two infirmary beds, and I'm on the other, everyone else crowded into the room. We've been stripped of all our tech and handed plain Afro U jumpsuits. The medic put a blanket around my shoulders because I can't seem to stop shaking.

We're under guard, I guess, because nobody has worked out yet if we're heroes or villains. They sent a recon party to the ruins of Pax about an hour ago—the dust storm is finally clearing, and they reported that they can see debris everywhere.

"Do you think you could drink something?" asks a man with kind eyes, who I'm sure has told me his name at least twice already. "I'd like to get some supplements into you, for the shock."

I just hold my hands out, because I know if I take it from him, he'll go away, at least for a little. Nearby, a harried man is speaking to the woman who I think is the head of the base. She has the most beautiful dark brown skin and her braids are coiled into spirals. If the world hadn't ended, I think I'd find her absolute competency quite comforting.

"—I'm not sure, Administrator. I do know there are messages flying in every direction. FreyaCo, India, and Euro West are redeploying their satellites to get a look at the surrounding territory and see if there really are Graves troops positioned to move in. Seems like the big guys all finally found something they agree on."

"It's over for Graves," she agrees, adjusting her braids as she takes a screen from him, prepping for some kind of video conference.

"Hunter had nothing to do with it," I say, raising my voice so the administrator turns to listen. "Hunter Graves. He tried to stop them."

"That's true," Sabrina calls out, breaking off her own narrative. "He didn't know. He tried."

"Hunter Graves tried what?" the administrator asks, frowning her confusion.

"He tried," I repeat, because those words are all I have left to offer him now. I want everyone here to see him like I do. To understand who he was.

"How did he—wait, Hunter Graves is on Mars?" the administrator asks, her eyes widening.

"He—" But I choke, and as my voice gives out and my face crumples again, I see her understand.

Hunter Graves *was* on Mars.

Perhaps it doesn't matter to them—Pax is gone, Hunter is gone. But I want them to know who he was.

Sabrina's finally winding down, and I can see the energy leaching out of her as reality sinks in. We escaped Nico and Blue Braid, but whatever comes next won't be good for either of us—and everyone on her team is gone.

It'll be my turn for a debrief soon. I'll tell them I'm a hitcher. Maybe they'll deport me back to Earth. Somehow, I just don't care.

"Recon party's back, ma'am," someone calls from the door, and everyone turns toward the voice. I can't see anything through the sea of bodies, and suddenly, I don't want to. I hug my mug against my chest, huddling inside my blanket, shrinking back.

They wouldn't have retrieved bodies, would they? No, you'd need a big rover for that. But that would mean he's still out there somewhere, on the surface, and that's worse. He'd be so cold.

I'm so cold, despite my blanket.

There's a fuss rising by the door, voices growing louder, and the people near me shuffle as if someone's shoving their way through. Then individual protests start to make their way through the crowd.

"Who's—?"

"I thought—"

"But you can't—"

And then . . .

And then . . .

And then.

And then Hunter's ghost is standing in front of me. He's covered in sweat and grime, his warm brown skin sallow with exhaustion, his hair disheveled, his eyes shadowed. You'd think a ghost would get to come back looking however they liked. Or do they have to look like they did when they died?

"You don't get to choose?" I murmur, feeling like I'm floating on cottony clouds. "Seems unfair."

"What?" he asks, and something deep inside me starts to struggle awake. "Cleo?" he says as I stare at him, his expression slowly turning uncertain.

Like I'm dreaming, I slowly raise one hand, extending it toward him. I'm so sure my fingers will pass straight through him that when they come to rest against his solid chest, my heart nearly stops. "Wait," I rasp. "Wait, are you . . . ?"

And then he understands, and he flashes me that impossible grin of his, and it's like the sun coming out. "I'm right here," he says softly, those green eyes focused on nothing else in the world but me.

And I think my mug hits the ground, and then I'm launching myself at him, and my arms are around his neck as he staggers back. I tangle one hand in his hair to pull his lips to mine and lose myself in the kiss that comes next.

He's so warm, so solid, so *real*, and his arms are around me to keep me in tight against him, and I can taste my own tears, but I can't stop.

"I'm here," he whispers, when we finally break for breath, and he presses his forehead to mine, and I focus on that point of contact, on the feeling of his strong hands against my body.

"How are you alive?" I whisper. "The base blew. It blew early."

"I got outside," he murmurs. "In a pressure suit, with an air tank, like you showed me. You taught me how, Cleo. I got outside without about a minute to spare. Then I waited, and hoped my oxygen would last, and the cavalry showed up in time, lucky for me."

"What about . . ." I don't even know what I hope for his sister. And the Martian, I suppose. The Boxer. Grace. Even Mr. Chin-Up. I mean, of all of them, I hope Marguerite's dead. She was prepared to murder thousands of people. But I ache for what that will do to him.

"I don't know," he says quietly, pressing his forehead to mine, the words just for us. "It's possible she got the last rover working in time, but she had maybe two minutes to do it in? I—I think it's unlikely she managed it."

"I'm sorry," I whisper.

"Me too," he murmurs in reply. "For who she used to be, if not who she became."

Our next kiss is softer, gentler. Comfort and togetherness, answers rather than questions. He cups my face with one hand, and I take what I think might be my first deep breath in hours.

"I told them it wasn't you," I whisper. The crowd has coalesced around Sabrina, who's found a second wind and is answering more of their questions, and for at least a few moments, Hunter and I are on our own tiny island of two. "They know you're not responsible."

He glances up and past me to where one of the media screens shows his mother at a press conference, surrounded by reporters from every outlet in the solar system, their hands in the air with the frenzied energy of a mob of predators. The sound is on mute, but I can tell she's shouting, coming apart at the seams in front of our eyes.

"I still think I might be broke now," he murmurs, rueful. "There won't be much of a company left."

"What will you do?"

"I'm not sure," he admits. He drops his gaze—when I look down too, I realize he's still wearing his cuff. "Maybe it's time I joined your side," he continues. "See what good I can do with what I have left."

"Maybe we figure out what *our* side looks like," I whisper in reply. "We can probably leave that until after we've showered, though."

That wins me a proper smile. "You're probably right. You know, there is one thing I want to try, though, that I don't think can wait."

I tilt my head into his touch and find I'm smiling too. "What's that?"

His eyes gleam. "I did say that if we survived this, I was going to ask you out on a date."

Somehow, impossibly, a laugh escapes me. "And I told you I'd say yes, Hunter Graves."

And then I kiss him again.

Acknowledgments

Well, reader, we reached the end! What a ride! Whether this is the first of my books you've picked up or the twenty-second, thank you for reading. Without you, this trip to Mars wouldn't have been possible at all.

If you'd like to join me on my next adventure, then you can find my monthly newsletter at amiekaufman.com. It's my favorite way to stay in touch, and means you'll always know about new releases and what's happening behind the scenes.

When it comes to this story, however, no book is created by the author alone. So, if you'll permit me, a few quick thank-yous to the following people:

My wonderful agents at Adams Literary, as well as the foreign agents and translators who help bring my work to other countries.

My brilliant editor Melanie Nolan, as well as the publishing teams at Random House, Allen & Unwin, Hot Key Books, Casterman, Knaur, Listening Library, and my overseas publishers for their endless efforts in sales and marketing, production, copyediting, design, publicity, and beyond.

The immensely talented Zoë van Dijk for my gorgeous cover artwork.

The many booksellers, librarians, and reviewers who help spread the word about my books—I am grateful for every time you've invited a reader to one of my worlds.

Lili Wilkinson, P.M. Freestone, and Kate J. Armstrong for reading drafts of this novel and offering their wisdom. Marguerite Syvertson for her scientific expertise and the loan of her name, which I promise I borrowed because I like her! Meg Spooner, who helped carry all kinds of loads during the drafting of this book. The Council, always.

When writing, I am always guided by a series of readers who offer me insight on experiences different from my own. I am, as always, grateful for their time and care. I am also grateful, in this case, to my scientific advisors from various space-related entities, all of whom I have attempted not to horrify with the science in this book. Any mistakes are, of course, my own.

Thank you to the many friends who kindly see this extrovert through a job that's often solitary. I am grateful to all of you. And of course, most of all, thank you to every member of my family.

And finally, Brendan and Freya: You are my greatest adventure. I love you.

About the Author

Amie Kaufman is the *New York Times* and internationally bestselling co-author of the Illuminae Files and the Aurora Cycle, among others, and the author of the Isles of the Gods duology. Her award-winning work has been translated into nearly thirty languages. Amie has degrees in history, literature, law, and conflict resolution and is pursuing a PhD in creative writing. Raised in Australia and occasionally Ireland, she now lives by the sea in Melbourne with her family and an extremely large personal library. You can visit amiekaufman.com to subscribe to her newsletter.